Now, We Will Know Monk Ryōkan

Haiku Adapted from Ryōkan's Famous Tanka

[In English and Japanese]

Tatsuo Ebe

良寛さまとこどもたち（丸山正三・画）
Ryōkan and the village children

今こそ知ろう良寛さんを
良寛の名歌を俳句〔英文・和文〕に翻案

江部 達夫

12 Long day:
I bounced the temari ball
with the children all day long

永き日を子らと一日(ひとひ)を手毬つき

絵： Shōzō Maruyama (1912-2013) : Doctor and Artist,
a member of the Shinseisaku Society. Author's Uncle.

「たくはつ良寛像」隆泉寺本堂前
"The statue of begging Monk Ryōkan" at Ryūsenji Temple

良 寛 さ ん

　私は子供の頃、幼稚園や小学校の先生から、面白いお坊さんのお話を聞いた。その名は「良寛さん」、いろいろなエピソードがあり、楽しく聞いた。良寛さんのお話は絵本でも読んだ。子供たちと遊ぶのが好きで、情け深く、今でも満月をみると子供の頃に覚えた「盗人に取り残されし窓の月」と言う句が頭によぎるのだ。

　「良寛さん」の詩歌や書は斎藤茂吉（医師、歌人）や相馬御風（歌人、評論家）らの研究により、明治時代の終わりごろから大正時代にかけて、広く日本中に知られるようになり、更に教科書にも載り、子供たちにも親しみある存在となった。しかし平成時代になると、良寛さんは教科書から消え、今では50歳以下の方は良寛さんを知らないのではと言われている。

　川端康成が1968年にノーベル文学賞受賞の記念講演「美しい日本の私」で、良寛の短歌を五首紹介し、良寛さんは世界に知られるようになったと言う。川端はノーベル賞受賞講演で、「形見とて　何か残さん　春は花　山ほととぎす　秋はもみじ葉」を良寛の辞世の句として紹介している。

　良寛（1758－1831）は禅僧であり、芸術家（詩人、歌人、書家）であった。
　良寛は越後出雲崎に生まれ、少年期に漢詩、漢文を学び、18歳の時に出家、22歳の時から、備中の円通寺（現　岡山県倉敷市玉島）の国仙和尚の下で厳しい禅の修行に励んだ。34歳の時、国仙の死を機に諸国行脚の旅に出て、39歳の頃　越後に戻った。
　良寛は生涯寺を構えず、妻子を持たず、物質的には無一物に徹し、清貧の思想を貫いた。

　良寛は托鉢を生業とし、時に寄進も受け、子供たちとの遊びを楽しみ、村人たちと親しく交わり、地域の文化人とも交流した。「ひとり遊びぞ我は勝れる」と歌う程に芸術にも打ち込んだ。
　何よりも好きだったのは自然の中での暮しであった。めぐり来る季節の移

り変わり、桜や梅の花、野の草花、秋の紅葉にも思いをめぐらせていた。

　良寛の芸術：　和歌は短歌、旋頭歌、長歌を合わせて1600首に及び、中でも短歌は1400首余り。斎藤茂吉や吉野秀雄（歌人）は「万葉調の中の良寛調」と高く評価している。漢詩は600首余り、俳句は107句が知られている。

　良寛の書も多く残されており、日本の書聖と言われる空海（弘法大師）をもしのぐと絶賛されている。

　これらの芸術作品の多くは円通寺での修行が終わり、故郷越後に戻ってからのものとされている。

　良寛さんは自然の中で、生あるものすべてに慈愛の心を持ち、自身は温良にして厳正な生涯を送った。

　今、地球は人類の飽くなき欲望により、破滅に向かわんとしている。権力者の飽くなき野望は地上を荒廃させ、多くの人々を殺害している。

　地球上の全ての生き物が平穏に生存し続けるためには、良寛さんの生き方を少しでも学びたいものだ。

　この書を和文と英文で表したのは、良寛さんの心を多くの方々に知ってもらいたいと願う気持ちからである。

　短歌を俳句に翻案したのも、俳句はより短い言葉で真意が伝えられ、言葉の足りない部分を読者の想像力で自由に補うことができると思うからである。

Ryōkan, Buddhist Monk

When I was a child, my primary school teacher shared interesting stories of a monk named Ryōkan. I learned even more from picture books about him. My first impression of Ryōkan was a kind-hearted monk who engaged with children.

Even now, I sometimes remember a haiku I learned during my childhood when I see the full moon:

> By the thief
> the moon left behind
> in my window

Thanks to the studies of Mokichi Saitō (doctor and poet) and Gyofū Sōma (poet and critic), Ryōkan's poetry became widely known in Japan from the end of the Meiji period into the Taishō period. Moreover, the poetry was adopted in textbooks, so Ryōkan was widely known among school children as well. However, Ryōkan's stories disappeared from textbooks in the Heisei period, so it is now said there are no people under 50 years old in Japan who know who Ryōkan is.

When Yasunari Kawabata received a Nobel Prize in 1968, he gave a memorial lecture on "Japan the Beautiful and Myself." In his lecture, he reintroduced five of Ryōkan's tanka poems so that his poetry returned to the public eye and the world at large. He is quoted as saying:

> What shall be my legacy?
> The blossoms of spring,
> the cuckoo in the hills,
> the leaves of autumn.

This poem was credited as Ryōkan's death poem, a search for enlightenment.

Ryōkan (1758-1831) was a Buddhist monk and artist (poet, Tanka poet and calligrapher). He was born in Izumozaki in the Echigo region (present day Niigata Prefecture). As a boy, he studied classical Chinese and Chinese poetry. He became a monk at 18, and from the age of 22, he strictly practiced Zen Buddhism under the chief priest Kokusen at the Entsū temple in Bicchū (present day a part of Okayama Prefecture).

At age 34, he went on a cross-country pilgrimage after Kokusen's passing. He returned to his home in the Echigo region at the age of 39.

Ryōkan was never head monk of his own temple or ever married.

His material possessions were the bare essentials, but he never felt his life lacking. He was content with a modest and honest life.

Ryōkan lived begging for rice, and sometimes people of the villages and his friends donated foods, drinks, or other supplies. He often played games with village children, closely interacted with nearby villagers, and amicably associated with people of culture in surrounding regions.

He was also deeply absorbed in artistic pursuits such as writing tanka poems, once saying, "I am better at playing by myself."

Most of all, Ryōkan enjoyed nature. He had a special fondness for the change of the seasons, specifically plum and cherry blossoms, flowers blooming in fields, and the red and yellow leaves in fall.

Art of Ryōkan: Ryōkan composed a little more than 1,600 poems including Tanka poetry, Sedouka and long poetry in his life. Tanka poems constituted the largest amount, Ryōkan having written 1,400. Thanks to Mokichi Saitō and Hideo Yoshino (poet), Ryōkan's Tanka poems are highly regarded with the Manyō style. Moreover, he wrote over 600 Chinese style poems and 107 haiku. There were many writings left by Ryōkan which were thought to exceed Kūkai (Kōbōdaishi) who was called Japan's master calligrapher.

These works of art were almost all completed after he returned from Bicchū.

Even with a warm, open mind, Ryōkan was strict with himself. However, he had a tender heart for all things in nature.

The earth is now being destroyed by human desires. People in positions of power, motivated by greed, are waging wars at various locations around the world. At present, these conflicts are leading to the ends of countless people's lives.

Every person from every nation would benefit from examining the Zen Buddhist monk lifestyle of Ryōkan. By doing so, we may begin to understand the value and irreplaceability of nature and earth.

As this book will be written in both Japanese and English, I hope Ryōkan's life, teachings, art and philosophy will become more widely known. When I thought more deeply about why I adapted tanka into haiku, I concluded that haiku are not only shorter, but they lend themselves more freely to the reader's interpretation and imagination.

Tatsuo Ebe

目次 CONTENTS

序　Prologue ……………………………………………………………… 5
　　良寛さん
　　Ryōkan, Buddhist Monk

第一部.「良寛の名歌百選」翻案の俳句 ……………………………… 11
Part 1.　Haiku adapted from the Book "One Hundred Famous Tanka of Ryōkan"
　　第一部に寄せて ………………………………………………… 15

第二部.「良寛　こころのうた」（3部作）から
　　　　100首の歌の翻案の俳句 …………………………………… 117
Part 2.　One hundred Haiku selected and adapted from the Books
　　"Ryōkan Tanka Poems of Heart" (consisting of 3 collections)
　　第二部に寄せて ………………………………………………… 125

おわりに　Epilogue ……………………………………………………… 228

謝　辞　Acknowledgments ……………………………………………… 230

参考資料　Bibliography ………………………………………………… 232

第 1 部 / Part 1

「良寛の名歌百選」翻案の俳句

Haiku adapted from the Book
"One Hundred Famous Tanka of Ryōkan"

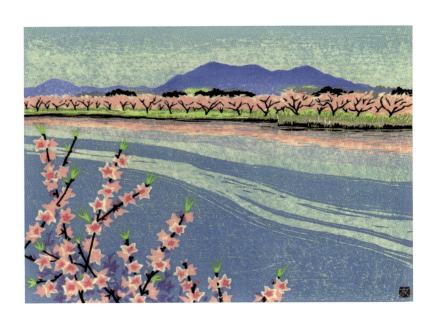

桃の花と中ノ口川
The peach blossom and
the Nakanokuchi river

6   The peaches in full bloom:
    the stream in the village
    reflects their colors

桃盛る里の流れは紅映し

3 Remembering
the children passed away,
no spring in my mind

亡くなりし子らを思へば春のなく

20   I feel pleasure
      on the day in spring,
      looking at flocking birds in play

      春の日に鳥群れ遊ぶを見る楽し

第一部に寄せて

　ここで俳句に翻案を試みた良寛の短歌百首は、谷川敏朗（選・解説）、小林新一（写真）両名の著書『良寛の名歌百選』（考古堂刊）によるものです。

　谷川氏によれば、個人の好みにより拾い出したものではなく、「過去に先達の方々が、良寛の代表作として評釈された中で、多く評論されている歌を選び出したもの」であるので、この百首の短歌は客観的に良寛の名歌と言えるものであると。

　良寛の詩歌には、移り変わる季節、人々の喜びや悲しみ、子どもたちと遊ぶ楽しみ、社会の在り方への嘆きなどに、誠の心が述べられている。歌の根底には、良寛の清貧に甘んじ、その中で生きて楽しみをも見出してゆく強い精神力が感じられる。

　良寛の短歌には季節感のないものもあり、俳句に求められる季語は、歌の背景より季節を推測した。短歌より十四文字も少なく表現することから、歌意を十分に伝えることが困難のものもあり、不足のところは読者の推量で補っていただければ幸いです。

　文章の形式は初めに翻案された俳句、次いで元歌とその歌意、歌より推し量った良寛の心情を和文と英文で表した。俳句と短歌の読みはローマ字で表した。

　The one hundred tanka poems of Ryōkan adapted to haiku in this book are taken from the book "One Hundred Famous Tanka of Ryōkan" written by Toshirō Tanikawa and Shinichi Kobayashi, published with Kōkodō.

　According to Mr. Tanikawa, who is selector and commentator of their book, these tanka poems were not selected by his own preferences, and he selected from representative tanka poems of Ryōkan that were commented on by many masters. So, the one hundred selected tanka poems are objectively representative of Ryōkan's tanka.

　In Ryōkan's tanka, he expresses his sincerity regarding the changing seasons, people's joy and sadness, the delight of playing with village children, his distress against immorality in the world, and other topics.

At the basis of Ryōkan's tanka, I can feel his mental strength in that he was content with a poor but honest life, and created many pleasures living a simple life.

It is necessary to write one seasonal word in one haiku. As there is no seasonal affair among Ryōkan's tanka, I made an effort to write a seasonal word from the background of the tanka as often as possible.

Moreover, haiku is shorter 14 kana words than tanka, so there is a prerequisite to imagine the background of the poem for the readers.

As the form of this writing, the haiku adapted from Ryōkan's tanka is first put on in English and Japanese, next Ryōkan's original tanka in Japanese and at last a meaning of tanka and Ryōkan's heart imagined by myself in Japanese and English.

The pronunciation of each haiku and tanka in Japanese is written in rōmaji.

1
> At the old temple in Tsu country,
> rain drops from cedar trees
> all night long
>
> 津の古寺に夜通し杉の梅雨しづく
> *Tsu no koji ni   yodōshi sugi no   tsuyu shiduku*

元歌　つの國の高野の奥の古寺に
　　　　杉のしづくを聞きあかしつつ

Tsunokuni no/ Takano no oku no/ furudera ni

sugi no shiduku wo/ kikiakashi tsutsu

歌意と良寛の心情　津國（摂津）にある古寺に泊めてもらった。梅雨の候の杉林に降る雨、その枝先から落ちる滴が板ぶきの屋根に夜通し響いて聞こえていたよ。

雨音に眠れなかった良寛、しかし快かったものと思われる。

Meaning of Tanka and Ryōkan's heart:
　Once a day I stayed at an old temple in Settsu country, and I heard the sound of rain dropping from the cedar trees onto the boards of the roof all night long.

　Ryōkan wasn't able to sleep through the night because of the rain's sound, but it's possible that his mind was at ease.

2
> The plum blossoms
> dropping on the ground,
> once floated in my sake cup
>
> 土に落つ酒に浮かべし梅の花
>
> *Tsuchi ni otsu　sake ni ukabeshi　ume no hana*

元歌　その上(かみ)は酒に浮(う)けつる梅の花
　　　　土に落ちけりいたづらにして

Sono kami wa/ sake ni uketsuru/ ume no hana
　　tsuchi ni ochikeri/ itaduranishite

歌意と良寛の心情　若かりし頃、梅の花を杯の酒に浮かせ楽しんだものだが、今はむなしく地に落ちているだけだよ。

良寛は地に落ちている梅花に虚しさを感じたのだ。

Meaning of Tanka and Ryōkan's heart:
　Looking at the plum blossoms on the ground, I remember the bygone days of enjoying them floating in my sake cup. Now, they are empty on the ground.

　Ryōkan may have felt a sense of emptiness seeing the plum blossoms that had fallen on the ground.

3
> Remembering
> the children passed away,
> no spring in my mind
>
> 亡くなりし子らを思へば春のなく
> *Nakunarishi   kora wo omoeba   haru no naku*

元歌　あづさ弓春も春とも思ほえず
　　　　過ぎにし子らがことを思へば

Adusayumi/ haru mo haru tomo/ omhoezu
　　suginishi kora ga/ koto wo omoeba

　あづさ弓（adusayumi）梓の木で作った弓（bow made of azusa tree）－「射る（iru-shoot）」、「張る（haru-draw）」から「春（haru-spring）」などに掛る枕詞（makurakotoba）。

　Makurakotoba is a set epithet used in Japanese waka poetry as an introduction.

歌意と良寛の心情　乳幼児の死亡の多かった時代、心浮き立つ春がやって来ても私には冬季に亡くなった子供たちのことを思うと、春を喜んでばかりはいられないのだ。

　良寛の子供たちへの愛情がよくわかる。

Meaning of Tanka and Ryōkan's heart:
　During a time when many babies and infants died, I couldn't experience the happiness from spring's arrival, because of the thought of so many children's death in winter.

　Ryōkan's loving heart toward children was expressed in this poem.

> 4   Looking at the children playing in spring,
> my tears flow
> remembering my dead child
>
> 遊ぶ子に亡子の思ひ涙の春
> *Asobuko ni　nakiko no omoi　nada no haru*

元歌　人の子の遊ぶを見ればにはたづみ
　　　　流るる涙とどめかねつも

　　Hitonoko no/ asobu wo mireba/ niwatadumi
　　　　nagaruru namida/ todome kanetsumo

にはたづみ（niwatadumi）－「流れる（nagareru-flow）」、「川（kawa-river）」などに掛る枕詞。

歌意と良寛の心情　春になり遊んでいる子供達を見ていると、亡くなった子を思い出して涙が出て来るよ。

　わが子を亡くした親の気持ちになって、涙して歌を詠んでいる良寛。

Meaning of Tanka and Ryōkan's heart:
　Looking at the children playing in spring,
　I couldn't stop the tears flowing from my eyes remembering my child that passed away.

　Ryōkan wrote a tear-filled tanka instead of the parents who lost their child.

5
> At the village in summer,
> I couldn't find my friend
> among men coming and going
>
> 夏の里往き来の人に君はなく
> *Natsu no sato　yukiki no hito ni　kimi wa naku*

元歌　この里に往き来の人はさはにあれども
　　　　さすたけの君しまさねば寂しかりけり
　　　　（この歌は五七七・五七七の形式の旋頭歌）

Konosato ni/ yukiki no hito wa/ sawani aredomo
　　　sasutakeno/ kimishi masaneba/ sabishikarikeri

　さすたけの（sasutakeno）－「君（kimi－emperor, head, you）」
に掛る枕詞。

歌意と良寛の心情　村里には往き来の人々は多くいるが、君の姿はもう見られないのだ。（良寛が五十歳の頃の夏、心の友であった三輪佐一が亡くなった。）

友を失った良寛の嘆き。

Meaning of Tanka and Ryōkan's heart:
　In the village there were many people coming and going, but from now on I will not find you among them.
　(When Ryōkan was 50 years old, Saichi Miwa, one of his good friends, passed away during summer.)

　Ryōkan expressed his grief about losing his close friend in this poem.

　The form of this poem is called Sedōka written by kana words forming of 577・577.

6
> The peaches in full bloom :
> the stream in the village
> reflects their colors
>
> 桃盛る里の流れは紅(べに)映し
> *Momo sakaru   sato no nagare wa   beni utsushi*

元歌　この里の桃の盛りに来て見れば
　　　　流れにうつる花のくれなゐ

Kono sato no/ momo no sakari ni/ kitemireba

nagare ni utsuru/ hana no kurenai

歌意と良寛の心情　桃の花盛りの時季にこの里に来てみると、川面には美しく花の紅が映えているよ。

　（この里の新潟市白根は江戸時代からの桃の名産地。そこには大河信濃川の分流中之口川が流れている。）

　良寛の心惹かれる光景だ。

Meaning of Tanka and Ryōkan's heart:
　　As I come to this village where the peaches are in full bloom, I can see the pink reflected in the river's surface.
　　(The Shirone area of Niigata city is a famous source of peaches, starting from the Edo period up to now where the Nakanoguchi river, a branch of the Shinano river, runs.)

　　Ryōkan was enchanted by the beautiful sight.

7
> As the memory of my mother,
> I look at Sado Island in summer
> every morning and evening
>
> 母が形見朝夕眺む夏の佐渡
> *Haha ga katami　asa yū nagamu　natsu no Sado*

元歌　たらちねの母が形見と朝夕に
　　　　　佐渡の島べをうち見つるかも

Tarachine no/ haha ga katami to/ asayū ni
　　Sado no shimabe wo/ uchimitsuru kamo

たらちねの（tarachineno）－「母（haha-mother）」に掛る枕詞。

歌意と良寛の心情　私は自身の故郷の出雲崎の浜から、大気の澄んでいる夏の朝夕、母の故郷の佐渡島を眺めるのが好きだった。
　（良寛の母は佐渡市相川の生まれ。）

年をとっても母への恋しさは変わらない良寛。

Meaning of Tanka and Ryōkan's heart:
　From the beach in my hometown of Izumozaki every morning and evening in summer, I like to look at Sado Island, the location of my mother's hometown.
　(Ryōkan's mother was born in Aikawa on Sado Island.)

In spite of Ryōkan's age, he still held his mother dear.

> 8　The rough rocky beach
> and Sado Island
> are always seen in summer
>
> 荒磯海と変はらず見ゆる夏の佐渡
> （ありそみ）
> *Arisomi to　kawarazu miyuru　natsu no Sado*

元歌　古へに変はらぬものは荒磯海と
　　　　向かひに見ゆる佐渡の島なり

Inishie ni/ kawaranumono wa/ Arisomi to

mukai ni miuru/ Sado no shima nari

歌意と良寛の心情　昔から変わらないものは、荒磯海（岩の多い海岸）と海の向こうに見える佐渡の島影であるよ。

良寛の心に刻まれた光景だった。

Meaning of Tanka and Ryōkan's heart:
　　The rough rocky beach and Sado Island seen beyond the sea remain for a long time.

　　They were always kept in Ryōkan's mind.

9
> Stretching legs in my humble hut,
> I hear the croaks of frogs
> from the rice fields among hills
>
> 庵(いほ)に足伸ばし山田の蛙聞く
> *Iho ni ashi　nobashi yamada no　kawazu kiku*

元歌　草の庵(いほ)に足さしのべて小山田の
　　　　　かはづの声を聞かくしよしも

Kusa no io ni/ ashi sashinobete/ oyamada no
kawazu no koe wo/ kikakushi yoshimo

歌意と良寛の心情　草庵の中、足を伸ばして、山の中の田から聞こえて来る蛙の鳴き声に耳を傾けていると楽しいよ。

良寛は長閑(のどか)な山里での生活が好きだった。

Meaning of Tanka and Ryōkan's heart:
　Stretching out my legs in the humble hut, I enjoy hearing the frogs croaking from the rice fields among the hills.

　Ryōkan liked living in peaceful mountain villages.

10 It's pleasant in the New Year
when sake, wasabi, and red-seaweed
are presented

酒山葵神馬藻届き春楽し
Sake wasabi   jinbaso todoki   haru tanoshi

元歌　神馬藻に酒に山葵に賜るは
　　　　春は寂しくあらせじとなり

Jinbaso ni/ sake ni wasabi ni/ tamawaru wa
haru wa sabishiku/ araseji to nari

歌意と良寛の心情　地の産物である神馬藻（赤藻屑…ホンダワラ科の海藻、お正月の飾り物に使用）にお酒、山葵を頂いて、一人で過ごす新春も寂しくはないよ。

友から届いた好きなものを目の前にして、春の訪れを楽しんでいる良寛。良寛は常々友人や村人たちに感謝の気持ちを持って暮らしていた。

Meaning of Tanka and Ryōkan's heart:
The New Year is happy for me because of many presented goods such as red seaweed, sake, and wasabi.

Ryōkan might be happy in the New Year and spring because of the goods presented to him by his friends. Ryōkan always lived with a sense of gratitude toward his friends and villagers.

11
> With your tasty sake
> I was drunk
> on the spring evening
>
> 君すすむうま酒に酔ふ春の宵
> *Kimi Susumu   umazake ni you   haru no yoi*

元歌　さすたけの君がすすむるうま酒に
　　　　　我酔ひにけりそのうま酒に

Sasutakeno/ kimi ga susumuru/ umazake ni
ware yoi nikeri/ sono umazake ni

歌意と良寛の心情　ある春の宵、私は良き友の一人の阿部定珍の館に出かけた。定珍の家は代々の酒造業、勧められるがままに美味いお酒を頂き、すっかり酔ってしまった。

好きなお酒には、良寛も自制が効かなかったようだ。

Meaning of Tanka and Ryōkan's heart:
　　One spring evening, I called on Sadayoshi Abe (one of Ryōkan's close friends, whose family had been running a sake brewery for generations), and he recommended delicious sake, so I got completely drunk.

　　Even Ryōkan couldn't control himself when it came to his favorite sake.

12　Long day :
I bounced the *temari* ball
with the children all day long

永き日を子らと一日を手毬つき
　　　　　　　(ひと)(ひ)
Nagakihi wo　kora to hitohi wo　temari tsuki

元歌　霞立つ永き春日を子供らと
　　　　　　(はる)(ひ)
　　　　手毬つきつつこの日暮らしつ

Kasumitatsu/ nagaki haruhi wo/ kodomora to
　　temari tsuki tsutsu/ konohi kurashitsu

霞立つ（kasumitatsu）－「春日（Kasuga－奈良市にある地名」
に掛る枕詞。転じて「春日（haruhi-spring day）」にも掛る枕詞
に。

歌意と良寛の心情　子供たちと遊ぶことが好きな良寛、だんだん日が
永くなって行く春の一日を、手毬を突きながら過ごしてしまったよ。

良寛には満足な一日であったようだ。

Meaning of Tanka and Ryōkan's heart:
　　As I enjoyed playing games with the children, I spent the entire day bouncing the *temari* ball on a long spring day.

　　It would have been an enjoyable day for Ryōkan.

　　Temari ball is one type of hand ball made of a cotton core wound tightly with cotton string.

> 13 With the children
> walking hand in hand
> gather the young greens
>
> 子供らと手をたづさへて若菜摘む
> *Kodomora to   te wo tadusaete   wakana tsumu*

元歌　子供らと手たづさはりて春の野に
　　　　若菜を摘めば楽しくあるかな

   Kodomora to/ te tadusawarite/ haru no no ni
     wakana wo tsumeba/ tanoshiku arukana

歌意と良寛の心情　子供たちと手を携え春の野に出て、若菜を摘んでいると楽しいよ。

年をとっても、子供心を失わない良寛。

Meaning of Tanka and Ryōkan's heart:
  I feel so happy walking hand in hand with children picking wild young greens in a spring field.

  Ryōkan retained his youthful mindset even though he was getting old.

14
> In the field picking young greens
> I recalled the past days
> by the cries of pheasants
>
> 若菜摘む野に雉子(きじ)の声昔思ふ
> *Wakana tsumu　no ni kiji no koe　mukashi omou*

元歌　春の野に若菜摘みつつ雉子(きじ)の声
　　　　聞けば昔の思ほゆらくに

Haru no no ni/ wakana tsumi tsutsu/ kiji no koe
kikeba mukashi no/ omohoyurakuni

歌意と良寛の心情　春の野に若菜をつんでいると、雉子の鳴く声が聞こえて来た。私はその声に昔のことを懐かしく思い出していた。

Meaning of Tanka and Ryōkan's heart:

　　Picking fresh greens in the spring field, I heard the cries of pheasants, and so recalled days long passed.

　　Ryōkan reminisced about his childhood while in the field hearing the cries of pheasants.

> 15　Plum blossoms :
> dimly seen in the mountain village
> in early evening
>
> 梅の花ほのかに山里宵迎へ
> *Ume no hana　honoka ni yamazato　yoi mukae*

元歌　足引の此山里の夕月夜
　　　　ほのかに見るは梅の花かも

(びき)(この)(ゆふづくよ)

　　Ashibikino/ kono yamazato no/ yūdukuyo
　　　　honokani miruwa/ ume no hana kamo

　　足引の（ashibikino）－「山（yama-hill）」や「峯（mine-peak）」などに掛る枕詞。

歌意と良寛の心情　夕暮れを迎えた山里の村、夕月の中ほのかに見えるのは梅の花であるよ。

　　春の夕暮れ、良寛は一抹のわびししさを覚えた。

Meaning of Tanka and Ryōkan's heart:
　　On an evening under a new moon, plum blossoms are dimly visible at a village among the mountains.

　　Ryōkan felt a little lonely looking at plum blossoms that evening.

> 16　On a moonlit evening,
> blossoms of the wild pear
> are faintly seen
>
> 夕月夜(ゆふづくよ)ほのかに見ゆる梨の花
> 　*Yūdukuyo　honokani miyuru　nashi no hana*

元歌　あしびきの片山かげの夕月夜(ゆふづくよ)
　　　　ほのかに見ゆる山梨の花

Ashibikino/ katayamakage no/ yūdukuyo
honokani miyuru/ yamanashi no hana

歌意と良寛の心情　山にかかるように夕月が出ている。その中ほのかに見えるのは山梨の花だよ。

自然観察の好きな良寛、夕暮れまで楽しんだ。

Meaning of Tanka and Ryōkan's heart:
　Wild pear blossoms were barely visible in the evening on a hill with the light of the moon.

　Ryōkan who liked to observe natural phenomena enjoyed viewing the pear blossoms in the evening.

> 17　The season comes :
> the birds step on the plum blossoms
> and strew them singing
>
> 梅花ふみ鳥鳴き散らす時来たり
> *Baika fumi　tori naki chirasu　toki kitari*

元歌　梅が枝に花ふみ散らす鶯の
　　　　　鳴く声聞けば春かたまけぬ

Ume ga e ni/ hana fumichirasu/ uguisu no
　　　nakukoe kikeba /haru katamakenu

歌意と良寛の心情　梅の枝に花を踏み散らして鳴く鶯の声を聞くと、いよいよ春がやって来た思いがするよ。

花の蜜を吸いながら花をまき散らしている鶯を見て、春の到来を楽しんでいる良寛。

Meaning of Tanka and Ryōkan's heart:
　When I hear the songs of bush warblers from the plum trees, stepping and strewing their blossoms, I feel that spring has come at last.

　Ryōkan might have a good time on the coming spring day, looking at bush warblers sucking nectar from plum blossoms and strewing them.

18
Picking violets
I came back forgetting
my begging bowl on the roadside

菫摘み道に鉢の子忘れ来し
Sumire tsumi   michi ni hachinoko   wasure koshi

元歌　道の辺に菫摘みつつ鉢の子を
　　　　　忘れてぞ来しその鉢の子を

Michinobe ni/ sumire tsumitsutsu/ hachinoko wo
　　wasurete zo koshi/ sono hachinoko wo

歌意と良寛の心情　道端に咲いている菫を見つけた良寛、托鉢の行を忘れ菫を摘んで、鉢の子を道端に置き忘れて帰って来てしまったよ。だいじなその鉢の子を。

　修行を忘れ春を楽しんでしまった良寛。鉢の子を道に忘れてきたことを悔やんでいる。
　良寛は忘れた鉢の子を別の歌で「あわれ鉢の子」と歌い、また置き忘れた所に残っていた鉢の子を「とる人はなし　鉢の子あわれ」と詠んでいる。

Meaning of Tanka and Ryōkan's heart:
　On the way for begging, I found violets by the roadside. I began to pick them, forgetting my training and went home leaving my begging bowl on the roadside.

　Ryōkan had a pleasant time during spring neglecting his training, and then regretted having forgotten his begging bowl on the roadside.

　In another tanka, Ryōkan wrote about forgetting his begging bowl, referring to it as "my poor begging bowl," but he found his bowl at the same site he had left it, and wrote, "no one will take my bowl, poor begging bowl."

19 On the long day
I am comforted
with the woods in your garden

永き日にみ園の林心なぎ
Nagakihi ni   misono no hayashi   kokoro nagi

元歌 むらぎもの心はなぎぬ永き日に
　　　これのみ園の林を見れば

Muragimono/ kokoro wa naginu/ nagaki hi ni
koreno misono no/ hayashi wo mireba

むらぎもの（muragimono）－「心（kokoro-heart）」に掛る枕詞。

歌意と良寛の心情　だんだん永くなってゆく春の日、私は友人阿部家を訪れた。お庭の林を眺めていると、冬季に塞いでいた心もようやく和んで来たようだ。

雪国で暮らす人々の気持ちを良寛は代弁している。

Meaning of Tanka and Ryōkan's heart:
　　As the days of spring have been gradually becoming longer, I called on the Abes, some of my good friends. I felt comfortable looking at the woods in the Abe's garden.

　　Ryōkan's poem represented the feeling of many people living in the snowy part of the country.

> 20
>
> I feel pleasure
> on a day in spring,
> looking at flocking birds in play
>
> 春の日に鳥群れ遊ぶを見る楽し
> *Haru no hi ni   tori mure asobu   miru tanoshi*

元歌 むらぎもの心楽しも春の日に
　　　　鳥のむらがり遊ぶを見れば

Muragimono/ kokoro tanoshimo/ haru no hi ni
　　tori no muragari/ asobu wo mireba

歌意と良寛の心情　鳥たちが群れて遊んでいる光景に見とれ、春の日を心から楽しんでいるよ。

巡って来る自然界を楽しんでいる良寛。

Meaning of Tanka and Ryōkan's heart:
　I am enjoying looking at the little birds flitting around on a spring day.

Ryōkan felt happy when he could experience nature.

21 In a spring field :
from the village in mist
I hear a horse neighing

春の野のかすむ村里駒ぞ鳴く
Haru no no no   kasumu murazato   koma zo naku

元歌　春の野のかすめる中を我が来れば
　　　　遠方里に駒ぞいななく
　　　　（をちかた）

Haru no no no/ kasumeru naka wo/ waga kureba

ochikata sato ni/ koma zo inanaku

歌意と良寛の心情　霞のたつ春の野に来てみると、遠くの村里から馬のいななきが聞こえて来るよ。

　動物も好きな良寛、長閑な田舎で聴く馬のいななきも心地よく聞かれた。

Meaning of Tanka and Ryōkan's heart:
　Coming out of the mist in a spring field, I heard a horse neighing from some distant village.

　For Ryōkan, as a lover of animals, hearing the neighing of a horse might have been the perfect complement to the pastoral countryside.

> 22
>
> In the mountain,
> hearing the songs of bush warblers
> I am cutting firewood
>
> 鶯の声聞く山に薪樵り
> *Uguisu no   koe kiku yama ni   takigi kori*

元歌 薪こり此の山陰に斧とりて
　　　　いくたびか聞く鶯の声

Takigi kori/ kono yamakage ni/ ono torite
　　ikutabi ka kiku /uguisu no koe

歌意と良寛の心情　薪にするため山陰で斧で木を切っていると、幾たびか鶯の鳴き声が聞こえて来たよ。

田舎暮らしの中で、良寛は日常生活を楽しみながらやっている。

Meaning of Tanka and Ryōkan's heart:
　　While using a hatchet to cut trees for firewood on the side of a mountain, I often heard the songs of bush warblers.

Living in the countryside, Ryōkan enjoyed the labors of his daily life.

23　Over the mountains of Sado Island
the haze lying
the sea glowing by the setting sun

佐渡の山かすみたなびき海は燃ゆ
Sado no yama　kasumi tanabiki　umi wa moyu

元歌　佐渡島(さどじま)の山はかすみの眉ひきて
　　　　夕日まばゆき春の海原

Sadojima no/ yama wa kasumi no/ mayu hikite
　　yūhi mabayuki/ haru no unabara

歌意と良寛の心情　佐渡が島の山々は眉を引いたように霞がたなびき、春の海原は沈みゆく夕日に、まぶしく輝いているよ。

　良寛は夕暮れに対岸の出雲崎から佐渡島を眺めるのが好きだったようだ。

Meaning of Tanka and Ryōkan's heart:
　A haze resembling a furrowed brow lies over the mountains of Sado Island while the sea on this spring day is glowing with the setting sun.

　Ryōkan liked to view Sado Island from Izumozaki over the sea.

> 24 The songs of little cuckoos
> flitting through the tree tops,
> spring had passed away
>
> こずゑ舞ふ時鳥の声春の過ぎ
> *Kozue mau   hototogisu no koe   haru no sugi*

元歌 青山(あをやま)の木ぬれたちぐき時鳥
　　　　鳴く声聞けば春は過ぎけり

Awoyama no/ konure tachiguki/ hototogisu

nakukoe kikeba/ haru wa sugikeri

歌意と良寛の心情　林の木々の葉は青々として、そのこずゑの間を時鳥が鳴きながら飛びまわっているよ。その声を聞くと確かに春は過ぎ去っているよ。

　春が過ぎ去り、時鳥の鳴き声で夏が来ていることに気づかされた良寛。

Meaning of Tanka and Ryōkan's heart:
　Through the tops of green forest trees, little cuckoos are flitting and singing. Hearing those cuckoos sing means that spring has passed.

　Ryōkan was stirred awake by the songs of little cuckoos meaning that spring had already passed and summer would soon arrive.

25　Maybe flocking together,
no songs of the birds
until falling flowers of silk tree

連れ旅か鳥の声なく合歓の散る
Tsuretabi ka　tori no koe naku　nebu no chiru

元歌　相連れて旅かしつらむ時鳥
　　　　合歓の散るまで声のせざるは

Aitsurete /tabi ka shitsuramu/ hototogisu
　　nebu no chirumade/ koe no sezaruwa

歌意と良寛の心情　時鳥は連れ立って旅に出かけているのだろうか。合歓の花の散る頃になっても声のしないのは。

　合歓の花の散る仲夏の候になってもやって来ない時鳥を心配している良寛。

Meaning of Tanka and Ryōkan's heart:
　Little cuckoos may be flocking together because they aren't singing, though summer is advancing and the silk tree flowers are falling.

　Ryōkan is concerned about the little cuckoos not returning until the middle of summer.

26　The village singing many birds
has changed into
the croaks of frogs

もも鳥鳴く里は蛙(かはず)の声となり
Momodori naku　sato wa kawazu no　koe to nari

元歌　もも鳥の鳴く山里はいつしかも
　　　　かはずのこゑとなりにけるかな

Momodori no/ naku yamazato wa/ itsushikamo
kawazu no koe to/ narinikeru kana

歌意と良寛の心情　山里の村は、春には多くの鳥たちが鳴いていたのに、いつの間にか蛙の鳴き声に変わっていたよ。

　自然界を見回すと季節はいつの間にか移り変わって行くものと感じている良寛。

Meaning of Tanka and Ryōkan's heart:
　In the mountain villages, many birds were singing in spring; however, without noticing, the bird songs changed into frogs croaking.

　Looking around nature, Ryōkan witnessed the gradual change of the seasons.

27
> This evening :
> I hear the croaks of distant frogs too
> in the mountain rice fields
>
> 山田鳴く蛙の遠音この夕べ
> *Yamada naku   kawazu no tōne   kono yūbe*

元歌　あしびきの山田の田居に鳴く蛙
　　　　声のはるけきこの夕べかも

Ashibikino/ yamada no tai ni/ naku kawazu
koe no harukeki/ kono yūbe kamo

歌意と良寛の心情　山の田圃で鳴いている蛙たち、この夕べは遠くからの声も聞こえて来るよ。

静かな夕べ、良寛は耳を澄ませて聴き入ったのであろう。

Meaning of Tanka and Ryōkan's heart:
　　Ryōkan heard frogs croaking both in the rice fields among the hills as well as the ones further in the distance this evening.

　　In the silent evening, Ryōkan might have strained his ears to catch the frogs croaking from far away.

28
Some sunshine in early summer rain :
the breeze blows
over the green rice fields

五月雨(さみだれ)の晴れ間の青田風渡る
Samidare no   harema no aota   kaze wataru

元歌　五月雨(さみだれ)の晴れ間に出でて眺むれば
　　　　青田涼しく風渡るなり

Samidare no/ harema ni ide te/ nagamureba
aota suzushiku/ kaze wataru nari

歌意と良寛の心情　降り続いた五月雨の晴れ間に庵から出てあたりを眺めると、青々とした田に涼しい風が吹き渡っているよ。

梅雨で庵にこもっていた良寛、晴れ間に外に出てみて清々しさを感じている。

Meaning of Tanka and Ryōkan's heart:
　　I looked around after going outside from my hut to see sunshine between the early summer rain, and I felt the cool breeze blow over the fresh green rice fields.

　　Going outside from his rain damp hut, Ryōkan felt a balmy breeze blowing over the green rice fields.

29
> Autumn is coming up :
> many plants begin to bloom
> at the hedge of my home
>
> 宿の垣百草(ももくさ)の咲く秋近し
> *Yado no kaki momokusa no saku aki chikashi*

元歌　我が宿の垣根に植ゑし百草(ももくさ)の
　　　　花咲く秋は近づきにけり

Wagayado no/ kakine ni ueshi/ momokusa no

hana saku aki wa/ chikadukinikeri

歌意と良寛の心情　私は宿の垣根にたくさんの草花を植えた。その草花が花を咲かせる秋が近づいて来たよ。

　秋に花を咲かせる草花も多い。その秋がいよいよやって来るのが楽しみな良寛。

Meaning of Tanka and Ryōkan's heart:
　　I planted many flowers at the hedge of my home garden. It is nearly autumn, so the garden flowers may begin to bloom.

　　There are many flowers that bloom in autumn, so Ryōkan looks forward to its arrival.

30

No one to whom
I will present boneset flowers
breaking off the stems

藤袴(ふじばかま)折りて贈らん人のなく
Fujibakama　orite okuran　hito no naku

元歌　秋の野に匂ひて咲ける藤袴
　　　　折りておくらんその人なしに

Aki no no ni/ nioite sakeru/ fujibakama

orite okuran/ sono hito nashini

歌意と良寛の心情　秋の野に咲き香っている藤袴、折って贈りたいのだが、私にはそのような人がいないのだ。

人恋しい良寛、だが贈りたいと思う人がいないのだ。

Meaning of Tanka and Ryōkan's heart:

There is no one to whom I want to offer a bouquet of fragrant boneset flowers that I picked from an autumn field.

This poem may have been written before Ryōkan met the nun Teishin.

| 31 | Let's sing and dance together :
can I sleep at the moonlight
this evening?

歌へ舞はむ今宵の月に寝られよか
　　　Utae mawamu   koyoi no tsuki ni   nerareyoka |

元歌　いざ歌へ我立ち舞はむひさかたの
　　　　　今宵の月に寝ねらるべしや

Iza utae/ ware tachimawan/ hisakatano
　　koyoi no tsuki ni/ inerarubeshiya

歌意と良寛の心情　さあ歌え踊ろうよ。今夜の名月に寝ていられようか。（良寛は踊りの輪の中で踊っている。）

良寛は村人たちに溶け込んでの盆踊りが好きなのだ。

Meaning of Tanka and Ryōkan's heart:
　　Let's sing and dance together all night long. How can I sleep during the harvest moon this evening?

Ryōkan liked Bon dancing together with the people of his village.

> 32　In the breeze and moonlight,
> let's dance all night long
> as a memory of my aging
>
> 風月いざ踊り明かさむ老い名残
> ふげつ
> *Hugetsu iza　odori akasan　oi nagori*

元歌　風は清し月はさやけしいざ共に
　　　　踊り明かさむ老いの名残に

Kaze wa kiyoshi/ tsuki wa sayakeshi/ iza tomoni

odori akasan/ oi no nagori ni

歌意と良寛の心情　風は清々しく、月は澄んでいる。
すがすが
さあ皆で踊り明かそう、私の老いの名残に。

晩年を悟っている良寛。

Meaning of Tanka and Ryōkan's heart:
　This evening there is a refreshing breeze blowing, and the moon is clearly shining. Let's dance all night long to the memory of my aging.

Ryōkan might sense that he is in his later years.

33
>
> In the village
> the sounds of drums and fifes,
> on the mountain the sounds blowing pines
>
> 里辺には鼓笛(こてき)に山は松の音
>
> *Satobe niwa   koteki ni yama wa   matsu no oto*

元歌   里辺には笛や鼓の音すなり
　　　　深山はさはに松の音して

Satobe ni wa/ fue ya tsudumi no/ oto sunari
　　　miyama wa sawa ni/ matsu no oto shite

歌意と良寛の心情　里の村は夏祭りで、笛や鼓の音でにぎわっているが、私の住む深山は松風の音が大きくしているよ。

　良寛は村里から聞こえて来る祭り囃しの音が好きだが、山の松風の音も好きだった。

Meaning of Tanka and Ryōkan's heart:
　In the village there are lively sounds of drums and fifes at the summer festival; however, in the mountains there are only the sounds of the wind among the pines.

　Ryōkan liked to hear the cheering sounds of festivals; moreover, he also enjoyed the sound of the wind among the pines.

49

34

In loneliness :
going out from my humble hut
there blows the wind in autumn

さびしさに庵(いほ)を出(い)づれば秋の風

Sabishisa ni   io wo idureba   aki no kaze

元歌　さびしさに草の庵(いほり)を出(い)で見れば
　　　　稲葉おしなみ秋風ぞ吹く

Sabishisa ni/ kusa no iori wo/ ide mireba
inaba oshinami/ akikaze zo fuku

歌意と良寛の心情　淋しさのあまりに、草庵(そうあん)を出てあたりを眺めてみると、稲葉を押しなびかせながら秋風が吹いているよ。

　一人暮らしの良寛、外に出て見ると、夏も終わり、秋の風が吹き始めている。ゆるやかに移りゆく季節を感じている。

Meaning of Tanka and Ryōkan's heart:
　　As Ryōkan felt lonely, he left his hermitage and looked around. He saw rice stalks being blown around by an autumn wind.

　　Ryōkan observed the gradual change of the seasons from summer to autumn.

35 　At the gate of my humble hut,
the crickets are singing
becoming colder night by night

わが門にこほろぎの鳴く夜寒かな
Waga kado ni　kōrogi no naku　yosamu kana

元歌　秋もやや夜寒むになりぬわが門に
　　　つづれさせてふ虫の声する

Aki mo yaya/ yosamu ni narinu/ waga kado ni
tsuduresase chou/ mushi no koe suru

歌意と良寛の心情　秋になり、しだいに夜寒になって来て、私の家の門のところでは、こおろぎという虫が鳴いているよ。

　だんだん夜寒になって行き、こおろぎの鳴く音が目立ってきた進みゆく秋、良寛は一抹の寂しさを覚えた。

Meaning of Tanka and Ryōkan's heart:
　As the nights become colder as autumn advances, the crickets sing at the gate of my humble hut.

　Ryōkan might have felt a little lonely in the advancing autumn in which the nights become colder day by day, and the songs of crickets stand out among the songs of other insects.

36　Through the night
a cricket has been singing
at my bedside

夜もすがらこほろぎの鳴く枕許
　Yomosugara　kōrogi no naku　makuramoto

元歌　しきたへの枕去らずてきりぎりす
　　　　夜もすがら鳴く枕去らずて

Shikitaeno/ makura sarazu te/ kirigirisu
　　　yomosugara naku/ makura sarazu te

　しきたへの（shikitaeno）－「まくら（makura-pillow）」や「とこ（toko-bed）」に掛る枕詞。

　江戸時代まで、「きりぎりす」は「こおろぎ」のこと。
Until the Edo period, crickets were called grasshoppers.

歌意と良寛の心情　私の枕元でこおろぎが一晩中去ることもなく鳴いていたよ。

　自然に溶け込む良寛、こおろぎの鳴く音も睡眠には心地良かったのであろう。

Meaning of Tanka and Ryōkan's heart:
At my bedside, a cricket was singing all through the night.

The songs of crickets might make sleeping comfortable for Ryōkan.

37　The autumn is lonesome
　　hearing a rainy sound
　　on the bamboo leaves

　　秋寂し笹降る雨の音聞けば
　　Aki sabishi　sasa furu ame no　oto kikeba

元歌　秋もややうら寂しくぞなりにけり
　　　　小笹に雨の注ぐを聞けば

Aki mo yaya/ urasabishiku zo/ narinikeri
ozasa ni ame no/ sosogu wo kikeba

歌意と良寛の心情　秋もしだいに寂しくなってきたよ。笹の葉に注ぐように降る雨音を聞いていると。

訪れる人のなくなる冬を前に淋しさが募る良寛。

Meaning of Tanka and Ryōkan's heart:

　　In the gradually advancing autumn, I felt lonely hearing the sound of rain falling on the bamboo leaves.

　　Ryōkan may feel more lonely before winter because no one is calling on him.

38　The stalks of Japanese pampas grass
are glowingly seen
here at the upstairs

薄(すすき)の穂輝き見ゆる高屋かな
Susuki no ho　kagayaki miyuru　takaya kana

元歌　秋の日の光り輝く薄の穂
　　　これの高屋に登りて見れば

Aki no hi no/ hikari kagayaku/ susuki no ho
　kore no takaya ni/ nobori te mireba

歌意と良寛の心情　高い家から眺めてみると、秋の日を浴びて薄の穂が輝いて見えるよ。

　日の光を浴びて白く輝いている薄の穂を見て、秋も半ばに来ていると感じている良寛。

Meaning of Tanka and Ryōkan's heart:
　Looking around from the upstairs of a house, the stalks of the Japanese pampas grass seem to glow in the autumn sunshine.

　Ryōkan might feel that it has become mid-autumn as he sees the Japanese pampas grass in the sunshine.

39
> The villages are in the mist,
> as I am on my way home
> surrounded by cedars
>
> 里は霧杉立つ宿への帰り道
> *Sato wa kiri   sugi tatsu yado e no   kaeri michi*

元歌 夕霧に遠路(をち)の里辺は埋(うづ)もれぬ
　　　　杉立つ宿に帰るさの道

Yūgiri ni/ ochi no satobe wa/ udumorenu
　　sugi tatsu yado ni/ kaeru sa no michi

歌意と良寛の心情　杉の木立に囲まれたわが宿への帰り道にながめると、遠くの村里は夕霧に埋もれていたよ。

霧の里は良寛には美しく見える夕暮れの景色であった。

Meaning of Tanka and Ryōkan's heart:
　On the way home in the evening, I found myself surrounded by a cedar grove, and I saw distant villages covered in mist.

　Ryōkan thought the villages covered by an evening mist were beautiful.

> 40　Wait for the moonlight
> and go home :
> your way home is not distant
>
> 月待ちて帰られ家路遠くなく
> 　　*Tsuki machite　kaerare ieji　tōku naku*

元歌　月よみの光を待ちて帰りませ
　　　　君が家路は遠からなくに

Tsukiyomi no/ hikari wo machite/ kaerimase

kimi ga ieji wa/ tōkaranakuni

歌意と良寛の心情　やがて月が昇るので、その明かりを待って帰られたらどうですか。あなたの家はそう遠くはないのだから。

　人恋しい良寛、訪ねて来た友人阿部定珍を少しでも長く引き止めたかった。

Meaning of Tanka and Ryōkan's heart:
　Although the moon will soon rise, you may leave here under moonlight because your home is not so distant.

　Ryōkan might want his friend Sadayoshi to stay longer because he misses him.

41
> You should leave here
> waiting for the rising moon :
> chestnut burrs on the mountain path
>
> 月待ちて帰られ山路毬が落つ
> *Tsuki machite　kaerare yamaji　iga ga otsu*

元歌　月よみの光を待ちて帰りませ
　　　　山路は栗の毬の落つれば

Tsuki yomi no/ hikari wo machite/ kaeri mase
　　yamaji wa kuri no/ iga no otsureba

歌意と良寛の心情　山道には栗の毬が落ちているので、月明かりを待ってお帰りなさい。

良寛の気遣う心がわかる。

Meaning of Tanka and Ryōkan's heart:
　　As there are chestnut burrs on the mountain path, you should wait for the moonlight before you leave.

　　This poem reveals Ryōkan's tender heart.

42 Coming over Mt. Kugami
leaves are falling at evening,
and I feel cool on my arms

国上越え木の葉の散る夕腕寒し
Kugami goe   konoha chiru yū   ude samushi

元歌　夕暮れに国上の山を越えくれば
　　　　衣手寒し木の葉散りつつ

Yūgure ni/ kugami no yama wo/ koekureba
koromode samushi/ konoha chiritsutsu

歌意と良寛の心情　夕暮れになり国上山の峠を越えて来ると、着物の袖に寒さを覚えるようになり、木の葉がさかんに散っているよ。

山では紅葉も散り始め、秋に終わりを告げようとしている。良寛は一抹の淋しさを覚えたのであろう。

Meaning of Tanka and Ryōkan's heart:
　In the evening, as Ryōkan was coming over the Mt. Kugami pass, he saw leaves falling and felt a coolness on his arms under his robe.

　Ryōkan might feel a little lonely as the winter season approaches.

> 43
> Even scarecrows
> are watching the birds
> picking the rice ears
>
> 案山子さへ穂拾ふ鳥を守(も)りてをり
> *Kakashi sae　ho hirou tori wo　morite ori*

元歌　あしびきの山田の案山子汝(なれ)さへも
　　　　穂拾ふ鳥を守(も)るてふものを

Ashibikino /yamada no kakashi/ nare saemo
　　ho hirou tori wo/ moru chou mono wo

歌意と良寛の心情　山田に立っている案山子でさえも鳥から稲を守ってやっているというのに。

　農民には感謝している良寛、案山子さえできる働きを自分にはできないと嘆いている。

Meaning of Tanka and Ryōkan's heart:
　Even the scarecrows standing in the rice fields are protecting the rice ears from the birds.

　Ryōkan is ashamed that he can't work for farmers even the scarecrows appear to be making an effort for them.

> 44 Please eat
> every remaining radish
> planted in the patch on the hills
>
> あさず食（を）せ山の畑に蒔きし大根（おほね）
> *Asazu ose   yama no hatake ni   makishi ōne*

元歌　あしびきの国上の山の山畑に
　　　　蒔きし大根（おほね）ぞあさず食（を）せ君

Ashibikino /Kugami no yama no/ yamahata ni

makishi ōne zo/ asazu ose kimi

歌意と良寛の心情　この国上山の畑に種をまいて育てた大根ですよ。残さずみんな食べてください、あなたよ。

　良寛は自給用に小さな畑で作った大根、友定珍に残さずに食べて欲しかった。

Meaning of Tanka and Ryōkan's heart:
　I want you to eat every last one of the Japanese radishes that I planted and grew in my patch of the hill.

　Ryōkan planted and grew Japanese radishes in his personal patch of Mt. Kugami for self sufficiency, so he wanted his friend Sadayoshi to eat every last one.

45
> As it pours rain every day in winter,
> I haven't gone out to villages
> begging for rice
>
> 日々時雨飯乞ふ里に出でずをり
> *Hibi shigure　iikou sato ni　idezu ori*

元歌　飯乞ふと里にも出でずこの頃は
　　　　時雨の雨の間なくし降れば

Iikou to/ sato nimo idezu/ konogoro wa

shigure no ame no/ manakushi fureba

歌意と良寛の心情　時雨が止むこともなく降り続くこの頃、托鉢にも出かけられず、庵に籠っているよ。

本格的な冬に向かう前に貯えが必要なのである。

Meaning of Tanka and Ryōkan's heart:
　　Since there were continuous showers in early winter, I couldn't go out to the villages to beg for alms and unwillingly stayed in my hut.

　　Before winter truly arrived, Ryōkan had to store rice and vegetables by begging.

> 46　In the winter rain,
> a stag is standing
> on the opposite hill
>
> 時雨る中雄鹿は立てり前の丘
> *Shiguru naka　ojika wa tateri　mae no oka*

元歌　やまたづの向かひの岡に小牡鹿(さをしか)立てり
　　　　神無月(かみなづき)時雨の雨に濡れつつ立てり
　　　　　　　　　　（旋頭歌）

Yamataduno/ mukai no oka ni/ saoshika tateri
　　Kaminaduki/ shigure no ame ni/ nuretsutsu tateri

　やまたづの（yamataduno）－「やまたづ」は「にわとこ（elder）」の古名－山たづの枝や葉は向かい合っていることから、「向かひ」、「迎へ」にかかる枕詞。

歌意と良寛の心情　向かいに見えるの丘の上に雄鹿が立っている。神無月の時雨の雨に濡れながら立っているよ。

　秋は鹿の繁殖の季節、丘の上に時雨に濡れながらじっと立っている雄鹿、連れ添う雌鹿のいないのに同情の念を持つ良寛。

Meaning of Tanka and Ryōkan's heart:
　On the opposite hill, a stag is standing drenched in the early winter rain on Kaminaduki(formerly October, now November).

　Ryōkan expressed his compassion for a stag with no hind, as deer rut during early winter.

> 47　In the rice fields at Iwamuro,
> a pine tree stands
> in the winter rain
>
> 岩室の田に立つ松の時雨けり
> *Iwamuro no　ta ni tatsu matsu no　shigurekeri*

元歌　岩室の田中に立てる一つ松の木
　　　　今朝見れば時雨の雨に濡れつつ立てり
　　　　　　　　　　（旋頭歌）

Iwamuro no/ tanaka ni tateru/ hitotsu matsu no ki
　　kesa mireba /shigure no ame ni/ nuretsutsu tateri

歌意と良寛の心情　岩室の田の中に立っている一本の松の木、今朝見ると時雨の雨の中に濡れて立っているよ。

時雨に濡れていることに同情している良寛。

この歌は旋頭歌（五七七・五七七の形式）であるが、次の「ひとつ松人にありせば傘かさましを蓑きせましをひとつまつあはれ」とつづくので、長歌の一部でもある。

Meaning of Tanka and Ryōkan's heart:
　　As I gazed out into the morning, I saw a lone pine tree standing in the Iwamuro village rice field showered in the winter rain.

　　Ryōkan worried about a pine tree showered in the winter rain.

　　This poem is followed by "If a pine tree is human, I will protect you with my paper umbrella or with my straw coat; what a pitiful pine tree," so it is a part of a long poem.

48
My hut is cold,
so I'll remain awake all night
burning firewood

庵(いほ)寒し夜(よ)は柴を焚き明かしたし
Io samushi　yo wa shiba wo taki　akashi tashi

元歌　山かげの草の庵はいと寒し
　　　　柴を焚きつつ夜を明かしてむ

Yamakage no/ kusa no iori wa /ito samushi
　　shiba wo takitsutsu/ yo wo akashiten

歌意と良寛の心情　山陰にある草ぶきの庵は大変寒いので、柴を炊いて夜を明かすとしよう。

寒い冬の夜は薪の火なしでは過ごせないのだ。

Meaning of Tanka and Ryōkan's heart:
　　As my thatched hut in the shadow of a mountain is very cold, I will spend the entire night burning firewood.

Ryōkan couldn't sleep on chilly winter nights without a fire.

49
> I lie putting my legs
> above the buried embers,
> however I feel a nip
>
> 埋（うづ）み火に足さし臥（ふ）すも寒さ染む
> *Udumibi ni   ashi sashiusu mo   samusa shimu*

元歌　埋（うづ）み火に足さしくべて臥せれども
　　　　今度（こたび）の寒さ腹に通りぬ

Udumibi ni/ ashi sashikubete/ fuseredomo

kotabi no samusa/ hara ni tōrinu

歌意と良寛の心情　炉の灰に埋めた火に足を延ばして寝ていても、この度の寒さは腹の底まで冷える寒さだよ。

良寛の住んでいた粗末な庵、寒さをしのぐのは大変だったのだ。

Meaning of Tanka and Ryōkan's heart:

　　I am laying down and putting my legs above the buried embers in hearth, but tonight's cold is unrelenting.

　　As Ryōkan lived in a hermitage, it was difficult to spend an entire day without heat.

> 50
>
> Standing and looking around
> on the slope of the shrine,
> it's snowing on the oak tree
>
> 宮の坂出で立ち見れば樫に雪
> *Miya no saka　idetachi mireba　kashi ni yuki*

元歌　この宮の宮のみ坂に出で立てば
　　　　み雪降りけり厳樫が上に

Kono miya no/ miya no misaka ni/ idetateba

miyuki furi keri/ itsukashi ga e ni

歌意と良寛の心情　この神社（燕市分水町の菅原神社）の坂道に出て立ち見渡すと、神聖な樫の木の上に雪が降っているよ。

神社の樫の木に降る雪、良寛には特別な思いがあったのだろう。

Meaning of Tanka and Ryōkan's heart:
　Standing on the slope of the shrine (Sugawara Shrine in Tsubame city) and looking around, I see that it's snowing on the holy oak tree.

　Falling snow on the holy oak tree at the Sugawara Shrine was thought to be special for Ryōkan.

51 Who would call on me
    making the path in snow
    piling up more and more?

    積もり行く雪踏み分けて誰か訪ふ
    Tsumoriyuku   yuki fumiwakete   tareka tou

元歌　今よりはつぎて白雪積もるらし
　　　　道踏みわけて誰か訪ふべき

Ima yoriwa/ tsugite shirayuki/ tsumorurashi

michi fumiwakete/ tareka toubeki

歌意と良寛の心情　これからは続いて雪が積もるようだ。そうなれば雪を踏んで誰が訪れてくれるだろうか。

深い雪の中誰も訪れて来なくなることを心配している良寛。

Meaning of Tanka and Ryōkan's heart:

From now on, the snow may be piling up more and more. Who will clear a path in the snow to call on me?

Ryōkan was worried that no one would visit him during winter.

| 52 | I haven't gone even to the villages
for begging rice,
since daily snow fall

飯乞ひに里にも出でず雪の日々
Iikoi ni   sato nimo idezu   yuki no hibi |

元歌　飯乞ふと里にも出でずなりにけり
　　　　昨日も今日も雪の降れれば

Iikou to/ sato nimo idezu/ narinikeri

kinōmo kyōmo/ yuki no furereba

歌意と良寛の心情　このところ毎日のように雪が降っているので、托鉢のために村に出て行くこともできないよ。

冬に備えての食糧の貯えが充分でなく、困り果てている良寛。

Meaning of Tanka and Ryōkan's heart:

It is snowing daily, so I haven't even gone to the villages to beg.

Ryōkan was worried about not having enough rice or other foods throughout winter.

53
> Snowing night:
> no sound in my humble hut
> made from cedar roof
>
> 雪の夜は杉屋根の庵音のせず
> *Yuki no yo wa　sugiyane no io　oto no sezu*

元歌　山陰の槙の板屋に音はせねども
　　　　　久方の雪の降る夜は著くぞありける
　　　　　　　　　　　（旋頭歌）

　　　Yamakage no/ maki no itaya ni/ oto wa senedomo
　　　　　　Hisakatano/ yuki no furuyo wa/ shirukuzo arikeru

　久方の（hisakatano）－天（tenn-sky）に関係のある「空（sora-sky）」、「月（tsuki-moon）」、「日（hi-sun）」、「雨（ame-rain）」、「雪（yuki-snow）」などに掛る枕詞。

歌意と良寛の心情　山の陰にある私の庵は杉板で葺いた屋根で、雨音はよく聞こえるが、雪の夜は音がしない。しかし何か気配を感ずるのだよ。

　風もなく雪の降る夜の静まり返った気配、雪国に住む人々にはよく分かる。

Meaning of Tanka and Ryōkan's heart:
　The roof of my hermitage in the shadow of a mountain is made of cedar board, so I don't hear sounds on snowy nights. However, I feel a presence on such a night.

　People living in snowy countries may have the same feeling as Ryōkan.

54
> Tomorrow the New Year,
> I can't sleep
> exciting in my mind
>
> 明日初春心ざわめき眠られず
> はつはる
> *Asu Hatsuharu   kokoro zawameki   nemurarezu*

元歌 何となく心さやぎて寝ねられず
　　　　明日は春の初めと思へば
なに　　　　　　　　　　　い

Nani to naku/ kokoro sayagite/ inerarezu
　　asu wa haru no/ hajime to omoeba

歌意と良寛の心情　何となく心が騒いで眠られないよ。明日が春の初めの日（新年）だと思うと。

指折り数えていた初春を迎え、嬉しさで心が騒いでいる良寛。

Meaning of Tanka and Ryōkan's heart:
　　I cannot get to sleep because I think tomorrow, New Year's, will be the first day of spring.

Ryōkan's mind is filled with joy, as tomorrow will be the new year.

55　Deeply snowing mount pass :
by what way did you come here
in my dream ?

雪深き山路を夢路たどり来し
　Yuki fukaki　yamaji wo yumeji　tadorikoshi

元歌　いづくより夜の夢路をたどり来し
　　　　み山はいまだ雪の深きに

Iduku yori/ yoru no yumeji wo/ tadorikoshi
　　miyama wa imada/ yuki no fukakini

歌意と良寛の心情　どこを通って夜の夢の中の道をここまでやって来たのだろうか。山はまだ雪が深く積もっているのに。

弟由之(ゆうし)が雪の中訪ねてきた夢を見た良寛、人が恋しいのだ。

Meaning of Tanka and Ryōkan's heart:

　As the mountain is still deep in snow, how did you come here tonight in my dream?

　Ryōkan had a dream about Yūshi, his younger brother, coming to him. He was lonely.

> 56　A zelkova tree in the garden
> is thought old
> by you and me
>
> 我も君も古きと思ふ庭の槻
> 　*Ware mo kimi mo　furuki to omou　niwa no tsuki*

元歌　我も思ふ君もしか言ふこの庭に
　　　立てる槻の木まこと古りけり

Ware mo omou/ kimi mo shikayū/ kono niwa ni

tateru tsuki no ki/ makoto furikeri

歌意と良寛の心情　友人定珍のお庭にある一本の欅、良寛も定珍ももう古い木になっていると言う。

樹齢を重ねた欅の古木、まだ元気に葉を茂らせているのに感心し、自分たちも老いには負けないぞと良寛たち。

Meaning of Tanka and Ryōkan's heart:

You and I think the zelkova tree in Sadayoshi's garden is old.

Ryōkan and his friend admired the zelkova tree remaining in spite of being an old tree, and their appreciation extends to not giving in to getting older.

| 57 | I will stay
at the hut surrounded
with the growing summer grass

夏草の茂れる庵にわれ庵る
　　　　いほ　　　　いほ　　　いほ
　　　　　　　　　庵る（仮の住まいを作って宿る）
　　　　　　　　　いほ

Natsukusa no　shigereru io ni　ware ioru |

元歌　　夏草は心のままに茂りけり
　　　　　　われ庵せむこれのいほりに
　　　　　　　　いほり

Natsukusa wa/ kokoro no mamani/ shigerikeri

ware iori semu /kore no iori ni

歌意と良寛の心情　　夏の草は思うがままに茂っている。その草の中にある庵に仮に住むことにしよう。

良寛は生い茂った夏草の中にある庵に涼しさを感じ、夏の間の仮住まいにしようと思ったのだろう。

Meaning of Tanka and Ryōkan's heart:

　　For right now, I will stay at the hermitage that is surrounded by growing summer grass.

　　Ryōkan may think that the thick and still growing summer grass will keep the hermitage cool during summer.

| 58 | The cottage in the Oto Shrine is quiet, so I have carried my cane

乙宮(おとみや)の下屋静けし杖移す

Otomiya no   shitaya shizukeshi   tsue utsusu |

元歌 乙宮(おとみや)の森の下やの静けさに
　　　　しばしとてわが杖移しけり

Otomiya no/ mori no shitaya no/ shizukesa ni
shibashi tote waga/ tsue utsushikeri

歌意と良寛の心情　乙宮(おとみや)（燕市の乙子(おとこ)神社）の境内の森にある小さな小屋が静かなので、しばらくそこで過ごそうと私の杖を移したよ。

静寂なところでしばらく過ごしたいと考えている良寛。瞑想の時間が欲しかったのだろうか。

Meaning of Tanka and Ryōkan's heart:
　As the cottage in the grove at the Otoko Shrine is quiet, I plan on spending some time there. So, I carried my cane there.

　It's likely Ryōkan hopes to spend some time in a quiet environment for the purpose of serene meditation.

59　A water running between mossy rocks
is clear,
also am I

岩間伝ふ苔水すみし我もまた
Iwama tsutau　kokemizu sumishi　ware mo mata

元歌　あしびきの岩間を伝ふ苔水(こけみず)の
　　　　かすかに我はすみ渡るかも

Ashibikino/ iwama wo tsutau/ kokemizu no
　　kasukani ware wa /sumi wataru kamo

歌意と良寛の心情　岩の間に生えている苔を伝って滴り流れている水が澄んでいるように、この世にひっそりと住む私の心もまた澄んでいるのだ。

この世にひっそりと住んでいる良寛の心は澄んでいる。

Meaning of Tanka and Ryōkan's heart:
　　As water running down between mossy rocks is clear, I also want clarity living quietly in this world.

　　Ryōkan living quietly in this world had a heart like flowing clear water.

> 60　The brave adults didn't weep,
> however cried looking at
> the cremated smoke in winter
>
> 大丈夫（ますらを）は泣けじ煙（けむ）見てむせぶ冬
> *Masurao wa　nakeji kemu mite　musebu fuyu*

元歌　大丈夫（ますらを）や伴（とも）泣きせじと思へども
　　　　煙見る時むせかへりつつ

Masurao ya/ tomonaki seji to/ omoedomo
　　kemuri miru toki/ musekaeri tsutsu

歌意と良寛の心情　強く勇ましい男子は共泣きしないと思うけど、火葬の煙を見る時にはむせび泣かずにはいられないことよ。

　葬儀の時には涙をこらえているが、火葬のけむりをみると大丈夫でも泣けてくるものだ。勇者でも人情は同じである。

Meaning of Tanka and Ryōkan's heart:
　The brave adults didn't weep at a funeral home; however, they cried when they saw the smoke of the cremation.

　The brave expressed their feelings as everyone else.

61　The birds coming
over the summer mountains
are singing this evening

夏の山越えて鳴く鳥この夕べ
Natsu no yama　koete naku tori　kono yūbe

元歌　夏山を越えて鳴くなる時鳥
　　　　声のはるけきこの夕べかな

Natsuyama wo/ koete naku naru/ hototogisu
　　koe no harukeki/ kono yūbe kana

歌意と良寛の心情　夏山を越えて時鳥が鳴いているよ。その声がはるか遠くに今夕は響いてゆくよ。

　この歌を詠んだころ、友人大村光枝がなくなった。
　大村光枝　信濃松代の藩士、国学者、五合庵に良寛を訪ねている（1754－1816）。

Meaning of Tanka and Ryōkan's heart:
　A little cuckoo was singing while coming over the mountains in summer, but the singing sounded far away this evening.

　Ryōkan's friend Mitsue Ōmura died just when this poem was written.

　Mitsue Ōmura (1754-1816)-A samurai of Matsushiro in Shinano Country (present day Nagano Prefecture) and Japanese literary scholar(poet). He visited Ryōkan at Gogōan and showed Ryōkan deep respect.

> 62 Living years on end,
> I could meet you again
> in this blooming spring
>
> 永らへて花咲く春にまた逢へり
> *Nagaraete   hana saku haru ni   mata aeri*

元歌　たまきはる命死なねばこの園の
　　　　花咲く春に逢ひにけらしも

　　Tamakiwaru/ inochi shinaneba/ kono sono no
　　　　hana saku haru ni/ aini kerashimo

　　たまきはる（tamakiwaru）－「世（yo－world）」、「命（inochi-life）」などに掛る枕詞。

歌意と良寛の心情　私の命が永らえたので、この園の美しい花が咲く春にまたお逢いできましたね。

　　梅の花が咲いている友人阿部家のお庭で、親しい人（定珍）と逢えたことを喜んでいる高齢の良寛

Meaning of Tanka and Ryōkan's heart:
　　Even though I have lived a long life, I could meet you again in this garden under the blooming plum trees in spring.

　　An aging Ryōkan was happy to meet a good friend (Sadayoshi) at Abe's garden under the full bloom of plum blossoms.

63　I am getting old,
　　however in this garden
　　the plum blossoms are in full bloom

　　我は老ゆこの園梅の盛りなり
　　　Ware wa oyu　kono sono ume no　sakarinari

元歌　この園の梅(むめ)の盛りとなりにけり
　　　　　わが老いらくの時にあたりて

Kono sono no/ mume no sakari to/ narinikeri
　　waga oiraku no/ toki ni atarite

歌意と良寛の心情　この家のお庭の梅が花盛りになったよ。私が年老いて来たこの時にあたって。

　年老いた良寛、梅の元気の良さに若かりし頃を思い浮かべているのだ。

Meaning of Tanka and Ryōkan's heart:
　Even though I have become older, the plum blossoms of this garden are in full bloom.

　Ryōkan remembered his prime while looking at the full bloom plum blossoms.

64 | Playing with the children
in the grove of the shrine,
don't grow dark this spring day

宮の森子らと遊びし春日暮れるな
Miya no mori　kora to asobishi　haruhi kureruna

元歌　この宮の森の木下(こした)に子供らと
　　　　遊ぶ春日は暮れずともよし

Kono miya no/ mori no koshita ni/ kodomora to
asobu haruhi wa/ kurezu tomo yoshi

歌意と良寛の心情　この神社の森の木陰で、子供たちと遊んでいる春の日は暮れないでほしいよ。

子供たちと一日中遊んでいたい良寛。

Meaning of Tanka and Ryōkan's heart:

　　As I am playing with the children in the shade of trees in the grove of the shrine, I wish that this spring day would never end.

Ryōkan wanted to spend all day long playing with children.

65
> Rice fields among hills in summer :
> an old man is carrying water
> all day long
>
> 山田夏小父(をぢ)はひねもす水運び
> *Yamada natsu　oji wa hinemosu　mizuhakobi*

元歌　あしびきの山田の小父(をぢ)がひめもすに
　　　　い行きかへらひ水運ぶ見ゆ

Ashibikino/ yamada no oji ga/ himemosuni
iyukikaerai/ mizu hakobu miyu

歌意と良寛の心情　山の田で老人が一日中、坂道を行ったり来たりして、水を運んでいる姿が見えるよ。

　山の田で老人が水運びのきつい労働をしている姿に感心している良寛。

Meaning of Tanka and Ryōkan's heart:
　In the mountain rice field, I saw an old man carrying water up and down all day long.

　Ryōkan might be moved by the old man working hard.

> 66
>
> While the late autumn rain is stopping,
> I'll draw water, cut firewood
> or gather greens
>
> 水汲みか薪伐り菜摘みか時雨る間に
> *Mizu kumi ka　maki kori na tsumi ka　shiguru mani*

元歌　水や汲まむ薪や伐らむ菜や摘まむ
　　　　秋の時雨の降らぬその間に

Mizu ya kuman/ takigi ya koran/ na ya tsuman
aki no shigure no/ huranu sono ma ni

歌意と良寛の心情　水を汲もうか、薪用に木を切ろうか、菜を摘んだりしておくか。晩秋になり、時雨が降り止んでるその間に。

冬支度に忙しい良寛。

Meaning of Tanka and Ryōkan's heart:

　　I'll draw water, cut firewood, or gather greens while the late autumn rain has stopped.

　　Ryōkan was busy preparing for winter.

67
> The light snow is falling
> on the Three Thousand Great Thousand Worlds,
> moreover falling in them
>
> あわ雪の三千大千世界の中またも降り
> *Awayuki no   MICHIOOCHI no naka   matamo furi*

元歌　あわ雪の中に立ちたる三千大千世界
　　　またその中にあわ雪ぞ降る

Awayuki no/ naka ni tatitaru/ MICHIOOCHI

mata sono naka ni/ awayuki zo furu

歌意と良寛の心情　泡のように溶けやすい雪が降る中に、三千大千世界（我々が住む世界の全体）が現出している。この一大世界の中に、また淡雪が降っているよ。

　雪国新潟の冬、白い雪がすべてを埋めて降っている中に瞑想しながらたたずみたいと思う良寛。

Meaning of Tanka and Ryōkan's heart:
　A light snow is falling on the Three Thousand Great Thousand Worlds (the whole of world in which we all living); moreover within them, the light white snow is falling.

　During the winter of snowy country Echigo (present day Niigata Prefecture), Ryōkan would be standing still in the falling snow, serenely meditating.

68
The night in winter rain :
is it dream or reality
that happened in days gone by?

過ぎしこと夢かうつつか時雨るる夜
Sugishi koto　yume ka utsutsu ka　shigururu yo

元歌　いにしへを思へば夢かうつつかも
　　　　夜は時雨の雨を聞きつつ

Inishie wo/ omoeba yume ka/ utsutsu kamo
　　yoru wa shigure no/ ame wo kikitsutsu

歌意と良寛の心情　夜になり時雨の雨音を聞きながら、過ぎ去った昔のことを思い出すと、それが夢であったのか、現実であったのか分からなくなるよ。

過去を振り返ってみて、夢か現(うつつ)かとまどう良寛。

Meaning of Tanka and Ryōkan's heart:
　Hearing the sound of early winter rain, it is difficult for me to parse the difference between dream and reality in the days that have gone by.

　Remembering the events of the past, Ryōkan was confused about what was a dream and what actually happened.

69
> The path of Buddha :
> I wish to realize even one day
> in a thousand years
>
> 法の道千歳に一日悟りたし
> のり　ちとせ　ひとひ
> *Nori no michi   chitose ni hitohi   satoritashi*

元歌　いかにして誠の道にかなひなむ
　　　　　　千歳のうちにひと日なりとも
　　　　　　　まこと

　　　　Ikanishite/ makoto no michi ni/ kanainan
　　　　　　chitose no uchini/ hitohi naritomo

歌意と良寛の心情　どうにかして仏の教えにかなえたいものだ。たとえ千年のうち一日だけであっても。

　長年苦行を積んで来た良寛でさえ、悟りはなかなか開けなかったようだ。

Meaning of Tanka and Ryōkan's heart:
　How can I live in a state of enlightenment for even a single day in a thousand years?

　Even Ryōkan, who had lived in a long period of practicing Buddhism, could hardly attain enlightenment.

> 70　Not departing from this world,
> I am better
> playing by myself
>
> 世離れずひとり遊びぞ我勝る
> *Yobanarezu　hitori asobi zo　ware suguru*

元歌　世の中にまじらぬとにはあらねども
　　　　　ひとり遊びぞ我は勝れる

Yononaka ni/ majiranu to niwa/ aranedomo
hitori asobi zo/ ware wa sugureru

歌意と良寛の心情　世の中の人々と付き合わないというのではないが、一人で遊んでいるのも楽しいよ。

良寛にとって一人遊びとは、本を読んだり、詩歌を詠んだり、書に没頭することである。

Meaning of Tanka and Ryōkan's heart:
　I sometimes felt out of touch with the world because I felt happy playing by myself.

　For Ryōkan, playing by himself might mean reading books, writing poems, or doing some writing.

> 71 Aging myself,
> I came home forgetting my cane
> on an autumn evening
>
> 杖忘れ帰る老いの身秋日暮れ
> *Tsue wasure　kaeru oi no mi　aki higure*

元歌　老いの身のあはれを誰(たれ)に語らまし
　　　　杖を忘れて帰る夕暮れ

Oi no mi no/ aware wo tare ni/ kataramashi

tsue wo wasurete/ kaeru yūgure

歌意と良寛の心情　年老いた吾が身の哀れさを、誰に語ればよいのだろうか。杖を忘れて庵に帰るこの夕暮れを。

年老いた良寛、物忘れが多くなったことを憂いている。

Meaning of Tanka and Ryōkan's heart:

　　To whom should I share the sadness of my old age? I came home having forgotten my walking stick on this autumn evening.

　　An aging Ryōkan worried about the tendency to forget and leave things behind.

> 72
>
> I will offer
> violets and dandelions in my begging bowl
> to the Buddhas of Three Worlds
>
> 鉢の子のすみれたんぽぽ三世仏に
> *Hachinoko no　sumire tanpopo　Miyobutsu ni*

元歌　鉢の子にすみれたむぽぽこき混ぜて
　　　　三世のほとけに奉りてな

Hachinoko ni/ sumire tanpopo/ kokimazete

Miyo no Hotoke ni/ tatematsuritena

歌意と良寛の心情　鉢の子に菫やタンポポを混ぜて入れ、三世にわたる仏様にさしあげたい。

三世は過去、現在、未来の世

Meaning of Tanka and Ryōkan's heart:

　　I wanted to offer both violets and dandelions in my begging bowl to the Buddhas of Three Worlds.

The 'Three Worlds' mean past, present, and future worlds.

73
Picking violets in the field,
I've spent the time
of begging for rice

托鉢も野にすみれ摘み時忘れ
Takuhatsu mo   no ni sumire tsumi   toki wasure

元歌　飯乞ふとわが来しかども春の野に
　　　　すみれ摘みつつ時を経にけり

Iikou to/ waga koshikado mo/ haru no no ni
sumire tsumitsutsu/ toki wo henikeri

歌意と良寛の心情　托鉢に出かけて来たのに、春の野に咲く菫の美しさに引かれ、長い時間を摘みながら過ごしてしまったよ。

修行よりも野辺の草花に魅せられた良寛。

Meaning of Tanka and Ryōkan's heart:

In spite of having gone out to beg for rice, I have spent my time picking violets in the spring field.

Ryōkan must have been charmed by the flowers of the field momentarily forgoing his ascetic practices.

74
My old home was desolate :
the garden and the hedge were covered
with the fallen leaves

郷は荒れ庭も籬も落葉覆ひ
Sato wa are   niwa mo magaki mo   ochiba oi

元歌　来てみればわが故郷は荒れにけり
　　　　　庭も籬も落葉のみして

Kitemireba/ waga furusato wa/ arenikeri
　　niwa mo magaki mo/ ochiba nomi shite

歌意と良寛の心情　久しぶりに私の育った故郷に戻ってみると、庭にも柴の垣根にも落葉が散り積もって荒れているよ。

　久し振りに故郷に戻った良寛、人の住まなくなった家、屋敷は荒れて、悲しく思っている。

Meaning of Tanka and Ryōkan's heart:
　When I returned to my old home after a long absence, I saw it had become quite desolate, the garden and hedge were all covered with fallen leaves.

　Ryōkan felt sad at the appearance of his desolate old home.

75
> Give me the laver
> grown in the seashore at Nodumi,
> not immediately
>
> 今ならず野積(のづみ)の浦の海苔賜へ
> Ima narazu　Nodumi no ura no　nori tamae

元歌　越の海野積の浦の海苔を得ば
　　　　　わけて賜はれ今ならずとも

Koshi no umi/ Nodumi no ura no/ nori wo eba
wakete tamaware/ ima narazutomo

歌意と良寛の心情　越後の海の野積の海岸で採れた海苔を手に入れたならば、分け与えてください。今でなくても良いので。（寺泊にいる妹に依頼した。）

良寛は春先の海岸の岩場で採れる岩海苔が好物であった。

Meaning of Tanka and Ryōkan's heart:
　　If you can get laver grown on the seashore at Nodumi in Echigo (present day Niigata Prefecture), when it's convenient for you I'd like to have a share of it. (Ryōkan begged for the laver for his younger sister living in Teradomari.)

　　Ryōkan liked Iwanori (a kind of laver) grown on the rocky seashore in early spring.

> 76　In the garden of your home
> coming by begging for rice,
> bush clovers are fully blooming
>
> **飯乞ひに寄る家の庭萩盛り**
> *Iikoi ni　yoru ie no niwa　hagi sakari*

元歌　飯乞ふとわが来てみれば萩の花
　　　　みぎりしみみに咲きにけらしも

Iikou to/ waga kitemireba/ hagi no hana
migiri shimimini/ saki ni kerashimo

歌意と良寛の心情　飯乞ひにこの家（阿部家）に来てみると、萩の花が庭いっぱいに咲いておることよ。（この場合、飯乞ふは定珍に食事「お斎（とき）」に呼ばれたもの。）

草花の好きな良寛、中でも萩は好みの花の一つである。

Meaning of Tanka and Ryōkan's heart:
　When I came to your home (the Abe's) to have a meal, I saw bush clovers aplenty in full bloom in your garden.

　While Ryōkan loved many flowers, above all, bush clover was one of his favorites.

77　Stuffing goose weed in my basket
on my way home at dusk,
I felt pity on departing fall

あかざ籠(こ)に帰る夕暮れ秋あはれ
Akaza ko ni　　kaeru yūgure　　aki aware

元歌　行く秋のあはれを誰に語らまし
　　　あかざ籠(こ)にれて帰る夕暮れ

Yukuaki no/ aware wo tare ni/ kataramashi
　　akaza ko ni rete/ kaeru yūgure

歌意と良寛の心情　秋も終わりになろうとしているもの悲しさ、誰に語ったらよいのだろうか。藜(あかざ)を籠に入れて庵に帰るこの夕暮れに。

　秋も暮れようとしている季節の変わり目、良寛にはもの悲しく覚えるのだ。

Meaning of Tanka and Ryōkan's heart:
　To whom can I tell of my sadness at fall's departure, as I travel home in the evening while stuffing some goose weed in my basket?

　Ryōkan lamented the departure of autumn.

78
I can't sleep in moonlit night,
so go out in the grove
of the temple

月夜には寝られずお堂の林へと
Tsukiyo niwa　nerarezu odou no　hayashi e to

元歌　月夜にはいも寝ざりけり大殿(おほとの)の
　　　　林のもとに行き帰りつつ

Tsukiyo niwa/ imo nezarikeri/ ōtono no
　　hayashi no moto ni/ yuki kaeritsutsu

歌意と良寛の心情　美しい月夜には眠りにつけなくて、お寺のお堂のそばの林の下を行ったり来たりしているよ。

煌々と夜空に輝く月、その月が好きな良寛、眠りにつけないのだ。

Meaning of Tanka and Ryōkan's heart:
　　I can't get to sleep on a night lit with a beautiful moon, so I am walking back and forth in the grove near the temple.

　　Ryōkan liked the brightly shining moon so much that he couldn't sleep well on the moonlit night.

79
> Bouncing the *temari* ball
> until ten times,
> it starts again and again
>
> 手毬つく十くり返しまた始む
> *Temari tsuku   tō kurikaeshi   mata hajimu*

元歌　つきてみよ一二三四五六七八九の十
　　　　十とをさめてまた始まるを

Tsukitemiyo/ hi hu mi yo i mu na ya/ koko no tō
　　　　tō to osamete/ mata hajimaru wo

歌意と良寛の心情　手毬をついてみなさい。一二三四五六七八九十とつき終えて、また繰り返し始まるように、仏の教えも限りないものですよ。
　「仏の教えに限りはない」と手毬を例に、良寛が貞心尼に返した歌。

Meaning of Tanka and Ryōkan's heart:
　Bounce the *temari* ball- one, two, three, four, five, six, seven, eight, nine, and ten times. Once you reach ten, it starts again and again. Also, there are no limits in Buddha's teachings.

　For Nun Teishin, Ryōkan wrote this tanka poem comparing Buddha's teachings to the *temari* ball game.

　貞心尼―（1798-1872）歌人、尼僧。晩年の良寛の心の友であり、良寛の最期をみとった。良寛の死後、良寛の歌や書、良寛と唱和した歌を一冊の本「蓮の露」として出版。

　Nun Teishin : (1798-1872) a nun and tanka poet. She was a spiritual and close friend of Ryōkan in his later years and present at his death. After his death, she published a book named "Hachisu no Tsuyu" (A Dewdrop on a Lotus Leaf). In this book she compiled Ryōkan's poems, the poems she and Ryōkan chanted, and Ryōkan's writings that he had left with his friends.

> 80
>
> In the night
> feeling cool on my arms,
> the moon is clear in the sky
>
> 衣手の寒き夜月の澄みわたる
> *Koromode no   samukiyo tsuki no   sumiwataru*

元歌　白妙の衣手寒し秋の夜の
　　　　月なかぞらに澄みわたるかも

Shirotae no/ koromode samushi/ aki no yo no
　　tsuki nakazora ni/ sumiwataru kamo

白妙の（shirotaeno）－白い布－「衣（koromo-robe）」、「月（tsuki-moon）」、「雲（kumo-cloud）」などに掛る枕詞。

歌意と良寛の心情　袖のあたりが寒いので外を眺めてみると、秋の夜空に月が明るく澄み渡って見えたよ。

心も澄み切っている良寛。

Meaning of Tanka and Ryōkan's heart:
　　I felt coolness on my arms this autumn evening, so I went out and looked at the sky. The moon was shining clearly there.

Ryōkan might be experiencing clarity similar to the autumn sky.

81 Come again in my humble hut
through the pampas grass
coated with dew

またも来よ尾花露分け柴の庵(いほ)

Matamo koyo   obana tsuyu wake   shiba no io

元歌 またも来よ柴の庵(いほり)をいとはずば
　　　　薄尾花(すすきおばな)の露を分けわけ

Matamo koyo/ shiba no iori wo/ itowazuba

　　susukiobana no/ tsuyu wo wakewake

歌意と良寛の心情　また来てくださいよ。このような柴造りの庵をいやと思わないなら、薄の葉や穂に降りた露をかきわけて。

良寛が貞心尼の再訪を促した歌。

Meaning of Tanka and Ryōkan's heart:

　Please visit again my hermitage if you don't mind, walking through the dew dampened pampas grass.

　Ryōkan wrote a tanka poem for Nun Teishin urging her to visit again.

82
> While you didn't call on me,
> the pass has been covered
> with the summer grass
>
> 君が訪(と)ふなきまま道は夏の草
> *Kimi ga tou   nakimama michi wa   natsu no kusa*

元歌　君や忘る道や隠るるこのごろは
　　　　　待てど暮らせどおとづれのなき

Kimi ya wasuru/ michi ya kakururu/ konogoro wa
　　　matedo kurasedo/ otozure no naki

歌意と良寛の心情　あなたが私のことを忘れたのか、夏草のため道が隠れてしまったためなのか、このごろは、待てど暮らせどなんの訪れもないことよ。

貞心尼の訪れの途絶えていることを嘆いている良寛。

Meaning of Tanka and Ryōkan's heart:
　Perhaps you have forgotten me, or perhaps the path to my home has been covered with summer grass, but these days, no matter how much I wait, you never come to visit.

　Ryōkan laments that Nun Teishin hasn't recently visited him.

83　You should regard a person
repaired the steep slopes
of the Shionori pass

塩之入(しおのり)の坂を直しし人偲べ

Shionori no　saka wo naoshishi　hito shinobe

元歌　塩之入(しほのり)の坂は名のみになりにけり
　　　　行く人しぬべよろづ世までに

Shionori no/ saka wa nanomi ni/ narinikeri
　　yuku hito shinube/ yorozu yo madeni

歌意と良寛の心情　塩之入(しおのり)峠は険しい坂道との噂だけで、今では通りやすい道に直されており、そこを通る人はいつの世にあっても、直した方を偲び、ありがたく思うように。

　「塩之入(しおのり)の坂」は与板と和島の間にある峠。この難所の峠を与板藩主井伊直経(いいなおつね)が改修した。

Meaning of Tanka and Ryōkan's heart:
　The slopes of the Shionori pass were once rumored to be steep, but a person repaired the pass creating an easier path for us, and every one who uses the pass should be thankful.

　The slopes of Shionori pass between Yoita and Wajima villages were repaired by Naotsune Ii, a feudal lord of Yoita.

84　Extended living moreover,
　　you had met such affairs
　　in winter

　　永らへてかかる憂き目を見る冬に
　　Nagaraete　kakaru ukime wo　miru fuyu ni

元歌　うちつけに死なば死なずて永らへて
　　　　かかる憂き目を見るがわびしさ

Uchitsukeni/ shinaba shinazute/ nagaraete
kakaru ukime wo/ miru ga wabishisa

歌意と良寛の心情　だしぬけに死んでしまったらよかったのに、死なずに生き永らえて、このようなつらい目を見ることの方が悲しいよ。

　文政11年（1828年）11月28日の三条大地震、その時の山田杜皋（とこう）への見舞状。良寛の死生観を示している。

Meaning of Tanka and Ryōkan's heart:
　It might be better to die suddenly than to stay alive and feel immense sadness seeing terrible events unfold.

　When the town Sanjou was hit by a devastating earthquake on November 28, 1828, Ryōkan wrote a letter of consolation for Tokō Yamada.
　This poem that was written in the letter might express Ryōkan's view of life and death.

85
> More than any gems
> your letter of early spring
> delighted me
>
> 初春の君が便りは玉よりも
> *Hatsuharu no　kimi ga tayori wa　tama yorimo*

元歌　天(あめ)が下に満つる玉より黄金より
　　　　春の初めの君がおとづれ

Amegashita ni/ mitsuru tama yori/ kogane yori

haru no hajime no/ kimi ga otozure

歌意と良寛の心情　この世に満ち溢れている宝玉や黄金よりも、春の初めに届いたあなたからの便りがありがたいよ。

良寛が貞心尼に送った歌。良寛の心情がよく分かる。

Meaning of Tanka and Ryōkan's heart:

　More valuable than any gems and gold in the world, the letter you sent in early spring delighted me.

　Ryōkan wrote a poem in reply to Nun Teishin in which his feelings for her are clearly expressed.

86
What I want dearly
is the top of turban shell
on the beach

恋しきは浜の栄螺の殻の蓋
　　Koishiki wa　hama no sazae no　kara no huta

元歌　世の中に恋しきものは浜辺なる
　　　　栄螺の殻の蓋にぞありける

Yo no naka ni/ koishikimono wa/ hamabe naru

sazae no kara no/ futa nizo arikeru

歌意と良寛の心情　この世の中で何よりも恋しいと思うものは、浜辺にある栄螺の殻のあの蓋だよ。

良寛は目薬を入れる壺の蓋にするために欲しかった。

Meaning of Tanka and Ryōkan's heart:

　　In this world, what I want dearly is the top of a turban shell on the beach.

　　Ryōkan wanted to use the top of the turban shell as the cover for a bottle of eye lotion.

> 87　Counting on my fingers,
> the spring days are
> already half over
>
> **指折りて数ふる春はもう半ば**
> *Yubi orite　kazouru haru wa　mou nakaba*

元歌　手を折りてかき数ふればあづさ弓
　　　　春は半ばになりにけらしも

Te wo orite/ kakikazoureba/ adusayumi
haru wa nakaba ni/ narinikerashimo

歌意と良寛の心情　指折り数えてみると、いつの間にか春はもう半ばになっていたよ。

　雪に埋もれた暮らしをしていると、いつの間にか春がやってきており、それも半ばを過ぎようとしているのに気づかされた良寛。

Meaning of Tanka and Ryōkan's heart:
　Only after counting on my fingers now did I notice that it is already the middle of spring.

　As Ryōkan has lived on a snowy mountain for a long time, he hadn't noticed the coming of spring.

> 88 Now, I don't know
> what may happen from tomorrow,
> drunken this spring day
>
> 明日からのこといざ知らず春の酔ひ
> *Asu kara no   koto iza shirazu   haru no yoi*

元歌　あすよりの後のよすがはいさ知らず
　　　今日の一日は酔ひにけらしも

Asu yori no/ nochi no yosuga wa/ isa shirazu
kyō no hitohi wa/ yoinikerashimo

歌意と良寛の心情　明日から後の生きて行く頼りとなるものはさあ分からないが、今日の一日はすっかり酔ってしまったよ。

　苦労をかけている弟の由之と酒盃を重ね、互いに歌を詠んでいる良寛、楽しい一日であった。

Meaning of Tanka and Ryōkan's heart:

　Since I'm not sure what tomorrow will bring, I have spent the entire day getting drunk.

　Ryōkan felt happy drinking sake with his younger brother Yūshi, and they wrote poems together in a light mood.

89　Father's handwritings :
recalling dear father still alive
tears blur my eyes in spring

父の書に在りし日思ひ涙(なだ)の春
Titi no sho ni　arishi hi omoi　nada no haru

元歌　みづぐきの跡も涙にかすみけり
　　　　在りし昔のことを思へば

Mizuguki no/ ato mo namida ni/ kasumikeri
arishi mukashi no/ koto wo omoeba

歌意と良寛の心情　父の書かれたものも、涙でかすんで来るよ。生きていた昔のこと思い出すと。

父の筆跡を見ると、生前の父を思い出し、涙でかすむ良寛。

Meaning of Tanka and Ryōkan's heart:
　　The things my father wrote become blurred with tears when I remember the time my dear father was alive.

　　Reading the writing of his departed father, Ryōkan's eyes naturally filled with tears.

> 90　As memories I would leave :
> blossoms, little cuckoos
> and colored leaves
>
> **我が形見花時鳥紅葉なり**
> *Waga katami　hana hototogisu　momiji nari*

元歌　形見とて何か残さむ春は花
　　　　夏ほととぎす秋はもみぢ葉

Katami tote/ nanika nokosamu/ haru wa hana
　　natsu hototogisu/ aki wa momijiba

歌意と良寛の心情　私は形見として何を残したらよいのだろう。春は花、夏は時鳥、秋はもみじ葉では。

良寛は人生の後半を越後の国（現、新潟県）の自然に囲まれて生活してきた。

Meaning of Tanka and Ryōkan's heart:
　I would like to leave something as memories: blossoms in spring, little cuckoos in summer, and colored leaves in autumn.

　Ryōkan had lived in nature at Echigo country (present day Niigata Prefecture) during the latter half of his life.

91　I feel pathos
in the first wind by which
the kudzu leaves are face and back

あはれさは葛の葉返す初風よ
Awaresa wa　kuzu no ha kaesu　hatsukaze yo

元歌　あはれさはいつはあれども葛(くず)の葉の
　　　　うら吹き返す秋の初風

Awaresa wa/ itsuwa aredomo/ kuzu no ha no
ura fukikaesu/ aki no hatsukaze

歌意と良寛の心情　ものの哀れを覚える物は、いつもそうだが、とりわけ葛の大きな葉を裏返しに吹き付ける秋の初めの風であるよ。（葛の葉は風に吹かれて裏返ると白っぽく見え、秋には赤紫色の花が房状に葉に隠れるように咲く。）

良寛は初秋に葛の葉を裏返すような風、またその頃の季節が好きだった。

Meaning of Tanka and Ryōkan's heart:
　　I always feel pathos is the first wind of autumn which exposes the upper and lower parts of the Kudzu leaves. (When Kudzu leaves are turned by the wind they appear whitish, and in autumn, they bloom in clusters of reddish purple flowers which are hidden by the leaves.)

　　Ryōkan liked the first early autumn wind as well as the season itself.

92
> The songs of crickets
> are languid to me,
> so don't just plant grasses
>
> こほろぎの鳴く音もの憂し草植ゑじ
> *Kōrogi no   nakune monoushi   kusa ueji*

元歌　今よりは千草は植ゑじきりぎりす
　　　　汝が鳴く声のいと物憂きに

Ima yori wa/ chigusa wa ueji/ kirigirisu
　　na ga nakukoe no/ ito monouki ni

歌意と良寛の心情　今からはいろいろな草を植えないことにしよう。きりぎりす（こおろぎのこと）よ、秋も深まるとお前の鳴く音がひどくつらく聞こえるのだよ。

　秋遅くまで鳴くこおろぎ、冬に近付くにつれ、数も少なく声も弱々しくなってゆく。虫の音も好きな良寛、良寛にはつらく聞こえるのであろう。

Meaning of Tanka and Ryōkan's heart:
　　I will not plant many grasses from now on because it is painful for me to hear the songs of crickets in late autumn.

　　Ryōkan loved the songs of insects in the fall, but the songs of crickets were painful for him to listen to because of the decrease in their number and the weakness of their singing getting near to winter.

93　　While I couldn't carry out my promise,
a season of the bush clover
passed away

契りしを果たせぬままに萩の過ぎ
　Chigirishi wo　hatasenu mamani　hagi no sugi

元歌　秋萩の花の盛りも過ぎにけり
　　　　契りしこともまだ遂げなくに

Aki hagi no/ hana no sakari mo/ suginikeri
　　chigirishi koto mo/ mada togenakuni

歌意と良寛の心情　秋の萩の花の盛りの時季は過ぎてしまったよ。あなたの所へ訪ねて行くという約束を果たさないままに。

　良寛は夏から始まっていた腹痛と下痢が秋になっても治まっていなかった。

Meaning of Tanka and Ryōkan's heart:
　In autumn, the full bloom bush clover has disappeared, but I couldn't carry out my promise to visit you.

　Ryōkan promised Nun Teishin that he would visit her home by autumn, but he couldn't carry out his promise because of his abdominal pain and diarrhea that lasted since summer.

> 94 If the pine trees at Yūgurenooka are humans,
> I would ask them
> the events of bygone days
>
> 夕暮れの岡松人なら昔問ふ
> 　*Yūgurenooka　matsu hito nara　mukashi tou*

元歌　夕暮れの岡の松の木人ならば
　　　　昔のことを問はましものを

　　Yūgurenooka/ no matsunoki/ hito naraba
　　　mukashi no koto wo/ towamashi monowo

歌意と良寛の心情　夕暮れの岡（燕市にある地名）に生えている松の木がもし人であったならば、昔のことを尋ねてみるであろうよ。

良寛は昔のことをいろいろ知りたかったのだ。

Meaning of Tanka and Ryōkan's heart:
　　If the pine trees growing at Yūgurenooka were humans, I would ask them about the events of bygone days.

Ryōkan wanted to learn the events of bygone days.

95　In autumn rain :
an old man is harvesting late rice
in the field among hills

秋雨（あきさめ）や山田の小父（をぢ）の奥手刈り

Akisame ya　yamada no oji no　okute gari

元歌　秋の雨日に日に降るにあしびきの
　　　　山田の小父（をぢ）は奥手刈るらむ

Aki no ame/ hinihini furu ni/ ashibikino
yamada no oji wa/ okute karuran

歌意と良寛の心情　冷たい秋の雨が毎日降り続く中、山の田で年老いた人が奥手の稲を今頃刈っているだろうよ。

　良寛は自分よりも年老いた方が雨の山中の田で、稲刈りをしていることに思いを寄せているのだ。

Meaning of Tanka and Ryōkan's heart:
　　As it's raining day by day in autumn, an old man may now be harvesting late rice in the mountain rice fields.

　　Ryōkan might be concerned about an older man working in the rainy rice fields in autumn.

> 96 Thankfully I get
> seven pomegranates
> on my hands
>
> ざくろ七個おし戴きぬ両(もろ)の手に
> *Zakuro nanako   oshiitadakinu   moro no te ni*

元歌   紅(くれなゐ)の七の宝をもろ手もて
　　　おし戴きぬ人のたまもの

Kurenai no/ nana no takara wo/ morote mote
oshiitadakinu/ hito no tamamono

歌意と良寛の心情　紅色の宝のような七個の柘榴をありがたく頭を下げ戴いた。人からの大切な贈り物であることよ。

　新津の桂氏の未亡人より弟由之を経て、頂いた柘榴への礼状に詠んだ歌。

Meaning of Tanka and Ryōkan's heart:
　Bowing thankfully, I'm carrying seven crimson pomegranates in my hands. They are treasured gifts from a person.

　This poem was written as a 'thank you' letter for a widow of Mr. Katsura from the town of Niitsu.

97

As soon as spring comes,
leave your hut and visit me
waiting for you

春来らば庵出で来ませ逢ひたきし
(はる く)　(いほ い)
Haru kuraba　io ide kimase　aitakishi

元歌　あづさゆみ春になりなば草の庵を
　　　　とく出て来ませ逢ひたきものを
　　　　　　　　　　(いほ)

Adusayumi/ haru ni narinaba/ kusa no io wo
toku dete kimase/ aitakimono wo

歌意と良寛の心情　暖かい春がやって来たならば、草庵を早く出て、お逢いしたくて待っている私のところを訪ねて下さいよ。

貞心尼に送った歌。来訪を待ち焦がれている良寛。

Meaning of Tanka and Ryōkan's heart:

As soon as spring comes, you must leave your thatched hut and visit me as I look forward to seeing you.

This poem shows Ryōkan's heart was sent to Nun Teishin urging her to visit as soon as possible.

98　Having diarrhea in summer,
I couldn't get the toilet
before defecations night and day

夏の下痢昼夜厠(かはや)に間に合はず
Natsu no geri　chūya kawaya ni　maniawazu

元歌　ぬば玉の夜(よる)はすがらにくそまり明かし
　　　あからひく昼は厠(かはや)に走りあへなくに
　　　　　　　（旋頭歌）

Nubatamano/ yoru wa sugarani/ kusomari akashi
　　Akarahiku/ hiru wa kawaya ni/ hashiri aenakuni

ぬば玉の (nubatamano) －「黒 (kuro-black)」や「夜 (yoru-night)」などに掛る枕詞。
　あからひく (akarahiku) －「日 (hi-day)」や「朝 (asa-morning)」などに掛る枕詞。

歌意と良寛の心情　暗い夜は途切れることなく、下痢をして明かし、明るい昼は厠に走っても、持ち堪えられないよ。

　良寛は亡くなる前年の夏に始まった下痢が治まらず、新年になり、1831年1月6日、74歳にて亡くなっている。

Meaning of Tanka and Ryōkan's heart:
　During the dark night, I was suffering from continuous diarrhea, and during the daytime, I couldn't get to the toilet before defecating.

　Ryōkan's diarrhea began in the summer and continued throughout the year without healing, and he died on January 6th, 1831 at the age of 74.

99
> As a person looking forward has come,
> we could meet again together.
> Anything else can I think moreover?
>
> **待ち人の来たり相見し何思ふ**
> *Machibito no　kitari aimishi　nani omou*

元歌　いついつと待ちにし人は来たりけり
　　　　　今は相見て何か思はむ

Itsuitsu to/ machinishi hito wa/ kitarikeri
ima wa aimite/ nanika omowan

歌意と良寛の心情　いつ来るか、いつ来るかと待っていた人がやっとやって来た。今このように対面できて、これ以上の何を思ったらよいのか。

病気のお見舞いに貞心尼が訪れ、無上の喜びを覚えている良寛。

Meaning of Tanka and Ryōkan's heart:
　　As the person I was waiting for, wondering when she would come, has finally arrived. Now that I can meet her like this, I can't imagine being happier.

　　Ryōkan could feel complete joy due to Nun Teishin's visit.

> 100
> Waiting for my last moment :
> I will take a trip in winter,
> so I stopped eating all
>
> 時を待つ身は冬の旅飯(いひ)を絶つ
> *Toki wo matsu　mi wa fuyu no tabi　ii wo tatsu*

元歌　うちつけに飯(いひ)絶つとにはあらねども
　　　　かつ休らひて時をし待たむ

Uchitsukeni/ iitatsu to niwa/ aranedomo
　　katsu yasuraite/ toki wo shi matan

歌意と良寛の心情　だしぬけに、食事を止めたわけではなく、身や心を楽にして、死期を迎えようとしているのだよ。

死を悟っている良寛、心は穏やかだった。

Meaning of Tanka and Ryōkan's heart:
　I haven't stopped eating, and I am waiting for my final moment at peace both in mind and body. I will pass away peacefully.

Ryōkan realized his death was imminent, and he was mentally at peace.

第 2 部
Part 2

「良寛 こころのうた」(3部作) から
100首の歌の翻案の俳句

One hundred Haiku Selected and Adapted
from the Books *Ryōkan Tanka Poems of Heart*
(consisting of 3 collections)

出雲崎良寛堂と佐渡島

Ryōkan Shrine at Izumozaki
and Sado Island

59 Under the clear sky
    Sado Island appears
    at the end of the sea

天高し海の果てなる佐渡が島

8   The murky world :
     the water of mountain stream
     cleanly flows

     濁る世や澄みて流るる谷の水

23   Plum blossoms :
      even if fallen
      be fragrant in my home

      梅の花散るとも香れ我が宿に

28 The falling snow in spring
    is mistaken
    as scattering cherry blossoms

    桜花散ると見まがふ春の雪

63   Like swaying sleeve
        the first ears of pampas grass
        beckon people

        初尾花袖ふるごとく人招く

93   Colored leaves fall always :
     for people
     an aging too

     紅葉散る人とて同じ老いのあり

99   Staying in my hut during winter,
     no traces of coming and going
     all season long

     冬ごもり宿に行き来の跡もなし

第二部に寄せて

　平成二十年は良寛生誕二百五十年にあたり、新潟日報社では全国良寛会の協力の下、平成二十年三月から三年間、新潟日報朝刊の第一面に、良寛の詩歌とその解説を「良寛」の表題で連載した。

　三年間で紹介された詩歌は千余首、その中短歌は七百余首あり、この歌から私の心に響いた歌百首を俳句に翻案を試み、英語にしてみた。記載の形式は第一部と同じである。

　これらの詩歌は「良寛　こころのうた」第１、２、３集の３部作として新潟日報事業社から出版された。

　In the year Heisei 20 (2008), on the 250th anniversary of Ryōkan's birth, Niigata Nippō Company serialized "Ryōkan" in the first page of morning newspaper of Niigata Nippō in that Ryōkan's tanka and other poems, and their explanations were carried for 3 years from March 2008, with the cooperation of the national Ryōkan's association.

　Among more than 1,000 poems carried in the newspaper for 3 years, more than 700 tankas were there. I adopted 100 tanka poems from these tankas that went straight to my heart.

　These tanka poems adopted were adapted to haiku and translated to English. The form of writing is the same as Part 1.

　These tankas and other poems were published with Niigata Nippō Business Enterprise as the books "Ryōkan Tanka Poems of Heart" consisting of 3 collections.

1
> The sky is clear :
> no words on Mt.Fuji
> in New Year's Day
>
> **晴れ渡る新春の富士言葉なし**
>   *Harewataru   shinshun no Fuji   kotoba nashi*

元歌　言の葉もいかがかくべき雲霞
　　　　晴れぬる今日の不二の高根に

　　Kotonoha mo/ ikaga kakubeki/ kumo kasumi
　　　　harenuru kyō no/ Fuji no takane ni

歌意と良寛の心情：　雲や霞もなく晴れ渡った今日の富士の嶺は、言葉では言い表せないほど美しい。

新年を迎え、良寛の心は晴れ渡っていた。

Meaning of Tanka and Ryōkan's heart:
　　There are clouds or mist in the clear sky, so Mt.Fuji appears beautiful beyond description.

　　Ryōkan's mind was clear on New Year's.

2
> In my home
> the painted rice cakes
> are put on Gods and Buddha
>
> 我庵は餅を絵に描き神仏に
> *Waga io wa　mochi wo e ni kaki　shinbutsu ni*

元歌　世の中は供へとるらし我庵は
　　　　餅を絵に描き手向けこそすれ

Yononaka wa/ sonaetoru rashi/ waga io wa
　　mochi wo e ni kaki/ tamuke koso sure

歌意と良寛の心情：　世の中はお正月には、神や仏さまに餅を供えているようだが、私の庵には何もないので、餅を絵に描いてお供えしよう。

質素な生活の中でも、良寛は新年の行事をおこなった。

Meaning of Tanka and Ryōkan's heart:
　In the world, people give rice cakes to Gods and Buddha during New Year's, but I don't have any in my hut, so my drawn picture of rice cakes will be my offering.

　Even though Ryōkan lived a humble life, he still held New Year's events.

3
> I feel lonely :
> a day in the New Year
> drawing to an end
>
> 心悲し初春の日の暮れゆけり
> *Kokoro kanashi   hatsuharu no hi no   kureyukeri*

元歌　むらぎもの心悲しもあらたまの
　　　　　今年の今日も暮れぬと思へば

  Muragimono/ kokoro kanashimo/ aratama no
    kotoshi no kyō mo/ kurenu to omoeba

　　むらぎもの（muragimono）－「心（kokoro-heart）」に掛る枕詞。
　　あらたまの（aratamano）－「年（toshi-year）」、
「月（tsuki-month）」、「日（nichi-day）」に掛る枕詞。

　　この短歌には二つの枕詞が使われており、「今年の今日も」
はお正月の一日と解釈した。

歌意と良寛の心情：　お正月の一日が、暮れてゆくと思うと惜しまれ
ることよ。

　　良寛には楽しみにしていたお正月の今日の一日が暮れて行くのが
寂しく思われるのだった。

Meaning of Tanka and Ryōkan's heart:
  It is sad to think that another New Year's Day will be drawing to an end.

  Ryōkan looked forward to this New Year's Day and felt sad it was coming to an end.

> 4 Getting old :
> with fire in room
> I feel cold by a draft
>
> 老いぬれば火あれどすき間風寒し
> *Oinureba   hi aredo sukimakaze   samushi*

元歌　　火と我とあれども寒しすき間風
　　　　　いづくも同じおいらくの身は

Hi to ware to/ aredomo samushi/ sukimakaze
izukumo onaji/ oiraku no mi wa

歌意と良寛の心情：　囲炉裏の火があっても、老いの身にはどこも同じく、隙間風は寒く感じられるものだよ。

与板町の酒造家山田杜皐(とこう)老から好物のお酒が届いた時の礼状の歌で、寒いときには体の中から温めるのが嬉しかった。

Meaning of Tanka and Ryōkan's heart:
　Even though there's a fire burning in the hearth, my old age means I always feel a draft from the cold.

　When it was cold, sake was the best remedy for Ryōkan to warm his body.

　This poem was written as a 'thank-you' letter to Tokō Yamada who was a sake brewer and sent sake to Ryōkan.

5
> Dreams :
> the past days are brief at present
> this world is also brief in future
>
> **今は昔来世は今ぞ夢の如**
> *Ima wa mukashi   raise wa ima zo   yume no goto*

元歌   古(いにし)へを思へば夢の世なりけり
　　　　今も来む世の夢にぞあるらむ

　　　　Inishie wo/ omoeba yume no/ yo narikeri
　　　　　　ima mo konyo no/ yume nizo aruran

歌意と良寛の心情：　昔のことを思うと夢のような世であった。今の世も過ぎ去ってみれば、夢のようにはかないことだろう。
　夢…はかないこと

人生は何時の世にあってもはかない夢のようなものだ。

Meaning of Tanka and Ryōkan's heart:
　When I think of the days passed away, it was like a dream, and I think real life is also as fleeting as a dream.

　Dream…a brief or fleeting matter (there is no precisely similar word in English)

　Ryōkan felt no matter what era of life you are in, it is like a fleeting dream.

6   How the wild ducks will spend
    in the snowing rice field
    tonight?

    田の鴨の今宵の雪にいかがせむ
    Ta no kamo no   koyoi no yuki ni   ikagasen

元歌 我が門の刈田の面にゐる鴨は
　　　　　今宵の雪にいかがあるらん

Wa ga kado no/ karita no omo ni/ iru kamo wa
koyoi no yuki ni/ ikaga aruran

歌意と良寛の心情：　私の庵の前に広がる刈田にいる鴨たち、今宵しんしんと降る雪の中、どのように夜を過ごすのだろうか。

良寛の慈愛の心は生あるもの全てに。

Meaning of Tanka and Ryōkan's heart:
　　I wonder how the wild ducks in the rice field before my hermitage will spend this evening while the snow steadily falls?

Ryōkan's compassionate heart was devoted to all living things.

7
> How many night do I sleep,
> counting the days
> until spring comes?
>
> 今いくつ寝ぬれば春来む月日よみ
> *Ima ikutsu　inureba haru kon　tsukihi yomi*

元歌　今よりは幾つ寝ぬれば春は来む
　　　　　月日よみつつ待たぬ日はなし

Ima yori wa/ ikutsu inureba/ haru wa kon
　　tsukihi yomitsutsu/ matanu hi wa nashi

歌意と良寛の心情：　冬の五合庵には訪れる人もいないので、今幾つ寝たら春が来るのだろうか。私は月日をよんで春を毎日のように待っているのだよ。

春、雪が消えた庵に、村人や子供たちがやってく来るのを楽しみに待っている良寛。

Meaning of Tanka and Ryōkan's heart:

No one visits my hermitage 'Gogōan' during winter. I spend every day counting the days until the coming of spring.

In the spring, once the snow has finally melted, Ryōkan looks forward to the villagers and children coming to his hermitage.

8   The murky world :
the water of mountain stream
cleanly flows

濁る世や澄みて流るる谷の水
Nigoru yo ya   sumite nagaruru   tani no mizu

元歌　濁る世を澄めともいはず我なりに
　　　　澄まして見する谷川の水

Nigoru yo wo/ sumetomo iwazu/ waga narini
sumashite misuru/ tanigawa no mizu

歌意と良寛の心情：　濁ってゆくこの世の流れを、澄めとは言わずによそ目に、だが谷川の水はおのずから澄んで流れてゆくよ。

　良寛の澄んだ心には、世の中からだんだん正しさが無くなってゆくのが憂えられるのだ。

Meaning of Tanka and Ryōkan's heart:
　I don't ask the murky stream of the world to be clear, but the valley stream flows clear all by itself.

　Ryōkan was worried that decency was slowly disappearing from the world.

9
> On the wings of wild geese
> flying across the cloud,
> the white flowers are falling
>
> 雲渡る雁の羽白き華の降り
> *Kumo wataru　kari no ha shiroki　hana no furu*

元歌　ひさかたの雲ゐを渡る雁がねも
　　　　羽白妙に雪や降るらむ
　　　　(はねしろたへ)

Hisakatano/ kumoi wo wataru/ karigane mo

hane shirotae ni/ yuki ya fururan

歌意と良寛の心情：　雲のある大空を渡ってゆく雁の白い羽に雪が降っているのであろう。

「如月末つ方なほ雪の降りければ」と詞書がついている。

二月（旧暦）末、北帰行の雁の姿を詠んでいる。

Meaning of Tanka and Ryōkan's heart:

　　Snow is falling on the white feathers of the geese as they glide across the cloudy sky.

　　A foreword was added to this poem: "Because of snowfall at the end of February (according to the lunar calendar)."

　　This poem was written at the end of February as the wild geese migrate to the Arctic.

10　After leaving the clouds over the back
and the mist in the valley,
the sunshine is there

峯の雲谷間の霞はる日差し

　　　　　　　　　　　はる…晴る、春の意

Mine no kumo　tanima no Kasumi　haru hizashi

元歌　峯の雲谷間の霞立去りて
　　　　　はる日に向ふ心地こそすれ

Mine no kumo/ tanima no Kasumi/ tachisarite
haruhi ni mukau/ kokochi koso sure

歌意と良寛の心情：　峯々の雲や谷間の霞もきれいに晴れて、おだやかな春の日差しになってゆく心地がすることよ。

春は心も晴ればれとしてくる良寛。

Meaning of Tanka and Ryōkan's heart:
　The clouds around the peaks and the mists in the valley have cleared, giving way to the gentle feeling of spring sunshine.

　Spring refreshes Ryōkan.

11
> No bloosoms of plum trees
> and no songs of bush warblers
> in your garden I came
>
> 梅咲かぬ鶯鳴かぬ庭に来し
> *Ume sakanu   uguisu nakanu   niwa ni kishi*

元歌　鶯もいまだ鳴かねば御薗生(みそのう)の
　　　　梅も咲かぬに我は来にけり

Uguisu mo/ imada nakaneba/ misonou no
　　ume mo sakanu ni/ ware wa kinikeri

歌意と良寛の心情：　鶯もまだ鳴いていないお庭、梅の花さえも咲いていないのに私は来ているのだ。

　この歌は良寛から、阿部定珍の「わが園の梅も咲かねばうぐいすもいまだ鳴かぬに君は来にけり」への返歌。御園生はここでは定珍のお庭。

春を待ちかねて友に会いに出かけた良寛。

Meaning of Tanka and Ryōkan's heart:
　I have arrived in the garden, but the songs of the bush warblers and plum blossoms haven't yet.

　This poem is a reply from Ryōkan to his friend Sadayoshi Abe's tanka poem: "You have come to visit so early in the spring, there are no plum blossoms or bush warbler songs yet."

　Ryōkan couldn't wait until a suitable time in the season to call on his friend for bird songs and plum blossoms.

> 12
> By some ties
> we all gathered at this home
> in the blooming evening
>
> えにしあり花の館に集ふ宵
> *Enishi ari   hana no yakata ni   tsudou yoi*

元歌　えにしあればまたこの館（たち）に集ひけり
　　　　花の緒（ひも）とく如月の宵

Enishi areba/ mata kono tachi ni/ tsudoikeri

hana no himo toku/ kisaragi no yoi

歌意と良寛の心情：　縁があってまたこの館（阿部家のお屋敷）に集まることができた。この如月（きさらぎ）（今の三月）の宵に梅の花が咲き始めたよ。

待っていた梅がようやく咲き始め、また皆と会えた良寛の喜び。

Meaning of Tanka and Ryōkan's heart:
　　By some coincidence we all gathered together in this home (the Abe Family mansion). On this evening in February (in the lunar calendar now March), the plum blossoms have begun to bloom.

　　Ryōkan was happy to meet his old friends in the Abe's garden under the plum blossoms.

13
> My old friend passed away :
> comfort my heart
> the plum blossoms!
>
> **古き友逝きて梅花よ心和（な）げ**
> *Furuki tomo   yukite baika yo   kokoro nage*

元歌　梅の花老いが心を慰めよ
　　　　　昔の友は今あらなくに

Ume no hana/ oi ga kokoro wo/ nagusameyo
mukashi no tomo wa/ ima aranaku ni

歌意と良寛の心情：　梅の花よ、老いてゆく私の心を慰めておくれ。昔一緒に花を見た友は今はいないのだ。

亡くなった友への寂しさを梅に話しかけている良寛。

Meaning of Tanka and Ryōkan's heart:

　Plum blossom, please comfort my aging heart. The friend with whom I once viewed the plum blossoms is no longer with me.

　Ryōkan talks to the plum blossoms to cope with the loneliness created by his friend's passing.

> 14 Wearing plum blossoms
> on my head
> remembered the past days
>
> 梅の花かざして過ぎしこと偲ぶ
> *Ume no hana　kazashite sugishi　koto shinobu*

元歌　梅の花折りてかざしていそのかみ
　　　　古りにしことをしのびつるかも

Ume no hana/ orite kazashite/ isonokami
　　furinishi koto wo/ shinobitsuru kamo

　いそのかみ（isonokami）－「古る（huru-old）」、「降る（furu-it's rain; it's snow）」に掛る枕詞。

歌意と良寛の心情：　梅の花を折って髪に飾り、昔のことを偲んでいるのだよ。
（良寛には髪の毛は無かったので、枝を折って背中に挿したのだろうか、または髪に飾ったと想像したのだろうか。）

　良寛は良き友たちと梅の花を髪に挿して遊んだ若き日を思い出している。

　この歌には「如月の十日ばかりに一人二人伴ひて槙木山に遊びたたりける。有則が元の家は跡形もなくて梅の花の盛りになむありければ詠める」との添書きがある。
　有則は原田鵲斎（じゃくさい）のこと。有則は分水町槙木山（現燕市）の庄屋に生まれ、医師で漢詩、和歌、俳諧に優れ、良寛と親

交があった。良寛より四年早く、六十五才で亡くなった。

Meaning of Tanka and Ryōkan's heart:

I picked plum blossoms and put them on my head, reminiscing about the past.

(Ryōkan had no hair, so perhaps he broke off a branch of plum tree and attached it to his back, or perhaps he imagined it as a garland on his head.)

Ryōkan recalls the days of his youth when he would play with close friends, wearing plum blossoms on their heads.

The poem is accompanied by the following note: "On about the 10th day of the second month, I went out to Makiyama with one or two friends. There was nothing built yet on the residential site of Arinori (a close friend of Ryōkan's), but the garden's plum blossoms were in full bloom."

Arinori: Jakusai Harada (1763-1827)
He was a doctor who excelled in Chinese poetry, tanka and haiku, and had a close friendship with Ryōkan. He died 4 years earlier than Ryōkan, at the age of 65.

15
> In my garden
> a bush warbler
> coming and singing
>
> 吾が庭に鶯の来て鳴きにけり
> *Waga niwa ni   uguisu no kite   nakinikeri*

元歌　うちなびき春は来にけり吾園の
　　　　梅の林に鶯ぞ鳴く

Uchinabiki/ haru wa kinikeri/ wagasono no
　　　ume no hayashi ni/ uguisu zo naku

歌意と良寛の心情：　うららかな春がやってきた。吾が庭の梅林に鶯が美しい声で鳴いているよ。

良寛は季節は春、花は梅、鳥は鶯が好きだった。

この短歌には季語になる言葉が三個あるので、俳句の原則である一句一季語に詠み替えるため、この歌の核心となる鶯に的を絞り、俳句に詠んでみた。

Meaning of Tanka and Ryōkan's heart:
　　A beautiful spring has come. In the plum grove of my garden, a bush warbler is singing beautifully.

　　Ryōkan liked spring the most of the four seasons, plum blossoms above other flowers and bush warbler among birds.

　　This tanka poem contains three seasonal words: spring, plum, and bush warbler. In order to follow the rules of writing haiku, I focused on bush warblers at the core of this haiku.

16
> A plum viewing party
> in full bloom tonight
> is regrettably at its end
>
> 盛りなる梅の宴の過ぐる惜し
> *Sakari naru   ume no utage no   suguru oshi*

元歌　梅の花いま盛りなりぬばたまの
　　　　今宵の夜半の過ぐらくも惜し

Ume no hana/ ima sakari nari/ nubatamano
koyoi no yowa no/ sugurakumo oshi

歌意と良寛の心情：　梅の花は今がまっ盛りだ。今宵の梅見の宴が夜も更けて、終わるのが惜しまれることよ。

梅を愛で、宴も好きだった良寛の心情がよく分かる。

Meaning of Tanka and Ryōkan's heart:
　　Plum blossoms are now in full bloom. Tonight's plum viewing has continued late into the night, and it will be regrettable to see it come to an end.

　　In this poem, Ryōkan's affinity for plum blossoms and plum blossom viewing parties can be understood.

> 17　Without a bush warbler's song
> the plum blossoms
> seen as snowing
>
> 鶯の鳴かずば梅花雪と見し
> *Uguisu no　nakazuba baika　yuki to mishi*

元歌　鶯の声なかりせば梅の花
　　　　こずゑに積もる雪と見ましを

Uguisu no/ koe nakari seba/ ume no hana
　　kozue ni tsumoru/ yuku to mimashiwo

歌意と良寛の心情：　鶯の囀りが聴こえなければ、梅の花を梢に積もる雪と見まがってしまうことよ。

見事に咲きそろった白梅の花、良寛は雪になぞらえている。

Meaning of Tanka and Ryōkan's heart:
　　If you couldn't hear the song of the bush warblers, you might mistake the plum blossoms snow for piling up on the tree branches.

　　Ryōkan compared white plum blossoms to snow piling up on the branches of plum trees.

> 18 Plum blossoms like snowing :
> no one notes them
> if not for their scent
>
> 雪のごと梅香らずば人知らず
> *Yuki no goto　ume kaorazuba　hito shirazu*

元歌　ふる雪にまがへて梅の花咲きぬ
　　　　香(か)さへ散らずば人知るらめや

Furuyuki ni/ magaete ume no/ hana sakinu
　　ka sae chirazuba/ hito shirurameya

歌意と良寛の心情：　降る雪と見まがうように梅の花が咲いている。香さえまき散らさなければ、人は気づかないでいるだろうよ。

梅の花に香りがあることを喜んでいる良寛。

Meaning of Tanka and Ryōkan's heart:
　Plum blossoms are blooming as if they were falling snow. If they didn't spread their fragrance, no one would know the difference.

　Ryōkan and many others enjoyed the sweet fragrance of plum blossoms.

| 19 | Plum blossoms :
getting older every year
I am lonely

梅の花老い行く吾のわびしけり
Ume no hana   oiyuku ware no   wabishikeri |

元歌   梅の花また来む春は咲くらめど
　　　　下降(したくだ)ちゆく我ぞわびしき

Ume no hana/ mata komu haru wa/ sakuramedo

shitakudachiyuku/ ware zo wabishiki

歌意と良寛の心情：　梅の花は春が来れば咲き香ってゆくのだが、年々老いてゆく我はわびしいものであるよ。

自然の偉大さに対して、人の世のはかなさを詠う。

Meaning of Tanka and Ryōkan's heart:

　　Although plum blossoms bloom anew each spring, I feel lonely as I get older and older.

　　Ryōkan compares the grandeur of nature to the loneliness of the human world.

20　Let birds sing :
the plum blossoms at my home
are now in full bloom

わが宿の梅いま盛りぞ鳥の鳴け
Waga yado no　ume no sakari zo　tori no nake

元歌　声立てて鳴けや鶯わが宿の
　　　　梅の盛りは常ならなくに

Koe tatete/ nake ya uguisu/ waga yado no
　　　ume no sakari wa/ tsunenaranaku ni

歌意と良寛の心情：　大きな声で囀ってくれ鶯よ。わが宿の梅今が盛り、いつまでも続くのではないのだから。

鶯の声と共に、花の盛りの短い梅を良寛は楽しみたいのだ。

Meaning of Tanka and Ryōkan's heart:

　　Let the bush warblers sing their song. In my home, the ephemeral plum blossoms are now in full bloom.

　　Ryōkan wanted to pass a pleasurable time enjoying the full bloom plum blossoms and the bush warbler's song.

21	Call on me :
	you can see the plum blossoms
	scattering by bush warblers
	訪ね来よ鶯散らす梅花見に
	Tazune koyo　uguisu chirasu　baika mini

元歌　心あらばたずねて来ませ鶯の
　　　　　木伝ひ散らす梅の花見に

Kokoro araba/ tazunete kimase/ uguisu no

kodutai chirasu/ ume no hana mini

歌意と良寛の心情：　もしよかったら訪ねて来ませんか。鶯が枝から枝へと伝って、散らしている梅の花を見に。

　鶯たちは花の蜜を吸っては花を散らしている。そんな光景を良寛は楽しんでいる。

Meaning of Tanka and Ryōkan's heart:

　Why not come and visit me? I will show you the bush warblers scattering the plum blossoms as they jump from branch to branch.

　Ryōkan perhaps enjoyed the scene of bush warblers sucking nectar from plum blossoms and scattering them.

22　It's blowing :
a bush warbler steps singing
along the branches of a tree

風の来て鳴くや鶯木伝ひに
Kaze no kite　naku ya uguisu　kodutai ni

元歌　風吹かばいかにせむとか鶯の
　　　　　梅の上つ枝を木伝ひて鳴く

Kaze fukaba/ ikanisemu toka/ uguisu no
　　ume no hotsue wo/ kodutai te naku

歌意と良寛の心情：　風が吹いてきたら花が散るので、鶯はいかにしようかと気をつかい、梅の木の高い枝を伝いながら鳴いているよ。

　梅の花が少しでも永く咲いていてほしいと思う良寛の心情を、鶯に託している。

Meaning of Tanka and Ryōkan's heart:

　When the wind blows, the plum blossoms scatter, so the bush warbler worries what to do and sings as it climbs into the upper branches of the plum tree.

　Ryōkan conveys his hope for plum blossoms to last as long as possible through the bush warbler.

> 23　Plum blossoms :
> even if fallen
> be fragrant in my home
>
> 梅の花散るとも香れ我が宿に
> 　*Ume no hana　chirutomo kaore　waga yado ni*

元歌　梅の花散りは過ぐとも我が宿に
　　　　香をだに残せ春の形見に

Ume no hana/ chiriwa sugu tomo/ waga yado ni
　　ka wo dani nokose/ haru no katami ni

歌意と良寛の心情：　梅の花よ、散ってしまっても我が宿に、春の形見としてせめて香だけでも残してほしい。

はかなく散ってゆく梅に語りかけている良寛。

Meaning of Tanka and Ryōkan's heart:
　Even though the plum blossoms have fallen, I hope they will at least leave their fragrance as a memento of spring.

Ryōkan speaks of the ephemeral nature of plum blossoms.

24
> In this home :
> as we seeing plum blossoms together
> not so regrettable even if fallen
>
> この宿に梅花相見し散らば散れ
> *Kono yado ni   baika aimishi   chiraba chire*

元歌 この宿に来(こ)しくも著(しる)し梅の花
　　　　今日は相見て散らば散るとも

Kono yado ni/ koshikumo shirushi/ ume no hana
kyō wa aimite/ chiraba chiru tomo

歌意と良寛の心情：　この家に来たしるしに、今日は一緒に梅の花を見れたので、もう何時散っても思い残すことはないよ。（粟生津(あおうづ)…現 燕市吉田…の医師鈴木桐軒の邸宅を訪ねた時のものか。）

　鈴木桐軒（1794 – 1851）は医業のかたわら詩文の才あり、良寛と親交があった。

　良寛晩年の歌。鈴木邸の盛りの梅を見て、もう思い残すことはないと思っている良寛。

Meaning of Tanka and Ryōkan's heart:
　As we could enjoy seeing plum blossoms together at this home today, no matter when they fall, I have no regrets.

　This tanka may have been written when Ryōkan visited Tōken Suzuki (1794-1851) at Aoudu village (present day Yoshida town in Tsubame city) who was a doctor and poet as well as a close friend of Ryōkan.

　This tanka is written in Ryōkan's later years.
　Looking at the plum blossoms in full bloom at the Suzuki residence, Ryōkan likely feels no regrets.

| 25 | At the foot of a hill,
picking dogtooth violets
want to eat them with children

山べ摘むかたこ食べたし子供らと
Yamabe tsumu　katako tabetashi　kodomora to |

元歌　あづさゆみ春の山べに子供らと
　　　　　摘みしかたこを食べばいかがあらむ

Adusayumi/ haru no yamabeni/ kodomora to
tsumishi katako wo/ tabeba ikakagaaran

歌意と良寛の心情：　春になって子供たちと山に行き、かたくりを摘んで食べたらどんなに楽しいだろうか。

春になったら子供たちと野山で遊びたい良寛。

Meaning of Tanka and Ryōkan's heart:

　　It will be pleasant to go to the foothills of the mountain with the village children, picking dogtooth violets and eating them.

　　Ryōkan looks forward to playing in the hills and fields with the children of the village once spring arrives.

26
> How to think about spring?
> If bush warblers have vanished
> from this world
>
> 鶯のたえて声なき世はいかに
> *Uguisu no   taete koe naki   yo wa ikani*

元歌   鶯のたえてこの世になかりせば
　　　　　春の心はいかにあらまし

Uguisu no/ taete kono yo ni/ nakariseba
haru no kokoro wa/ ikani aramashi

歌意と良寛の心情：　鶯が絶えてこの世からいなくなったら、春を迎える心はどうしようもなく淋しいだろうよ。

　梅と鶯が大好きな良寛、もしこの世から鶯がいなくなったら、春はどうなるだろうと心配する。

Meaning of Tanka and Ryōkan's heart:

　If bush warblers vanished from the world, my heart would be miserable waiting for spring.

　Ryōkan, who loved plum blossoms and bush warblers, might be worried about a spring season, without bush warblers.

27
Spring mist :
my heart is going ahead
for mountain and river

山川に心馳せさす春がすみ
Yama kawa ni　kokoro hasesasu　harugasumi

元歌　春がすみ立ちにし日より山川に
　　　　心は遠くやりにけるかな

Harugasumi/ tachinishi hi yori/ yama kawa ni
kokoro wa tōku/ yari ni keru kana

歌意と良寛の心情：　春になり、霞が立ち始めたその日から、山や川辺に心は馳せて行ってしまったよ。

永い冬も終わり、春がすみが立つと、良寛の心は大自然の変化に戸惑うて行くようだ。

Meaning of Tanka and Ryōkan's heart:
　　Since a day in spring and the mist began to rise, my heart was drawn to the mountains and rivers.

　　The changes of the seasons might have created conflicting sentiments for Ryōkan regarding the natural world.

28　The falling snow in spring
is mistaken
as scattering cherry blossoms

桜花散ると見まがふ春の雪
Sakurabana　chiru to mimagau　haru no yuki

元歌　　桜花降るかとばかり見るまでに
　　　　　　降れどたまらぬ春の淡雪

Sakurabana/ huru ka to bakari/ miru madeni
fure do tamaranu/ haru no awayuki

歌意と良寛の心情：　桜の花が散っているものとばかり見ていたら、降っても地には残らない春の淡雪であるよ。

　桜の季節、春の寒波が雪を運んでくることがある。良寛はこの雪を楽しんでいた様子がうかがえろ。

Meaning of Tanka and Ryōkan's heart:
　Though I thought I saw the scattering of cherry blossoms, it is lightly snowing which melts away as it hits the ground.

　During cherry blossom season, cold waves sometimes bring snow. Ryōkan might have enjoyed the snow.

> 29
>
> How to change blossoms
> in to dark and light colors
> in a single tree?
>
> いかにして濃き薄き花一つ木に
> *Ikanishite koki usuki hana hitotsu ki ni*

元歌 いかなれば同じ一つに咲く花の
    濃くも薄くも色を分くらむ

Ikanareba/ onaji hitotsu ni/ saku hana no
 koku mo usuku mo/ iro wo wakuran

歌意と良寛の心情： どうして同じ木に一緒に咲くのに、桜の花に濃いものや薄いものが生まれるのだろうか。

桜の僅かな濃淡の違いを不思議に思った良寛。

Meaning of Tanka and Ryōkan's heart:
 Why are there some cherry blossoms that are dark and others light, even though they bloom together on the same tree?

 Ryōkan might feel the change of cherry blossom colors on a single tree is mysterious.

30
>
> Since the coming of spring
> to my humble hut,
> my heart in the fields
>
> わが宿に春たちしより心野に
> *Waga yado ni   haru tachishi yori   kokoro no ni*

元歌　わが宿の軒端に春のたちしより
　　　　心は野べにありにけるかな

Waga yado no/ nokiba ni haru no/ tachishi yori

kokoro wa nobe ni/ arinikeru kana

歌意と良寛の心情：　私の家の軒端に春がやって来たその時から、わたしの心はもう野辺にあるようだ。

心が解放される春がやって来たことを実感している良寛。

Meaning of Tanka and Ryōkan's heart:

　From the moment spring arrives on the eaves of my hermitage, my heart seems to be in the fields.

Ryōkan realizes that the arrival of spring makes him feel free.

31
> Without notice,
> the fresh grasses in the field
> begins to sprout
>
> いつの間に野辺の若草萌え出づる
> *Itsu no mani　nobe no wakakusa　moe iduru*

元歌　あづさゆみ春はそれともわかぬまに
　　　　野辺の若草染め出づるなり

Adusayumi/ haru wa soretomo/ wakanumani
nobe no wakakusa/ some idurunari

歌意と良寛の心情：　春がやって来たのかどうかよく分からないうちに、野原の若草が萌え始めているよ。

良寛はいつの間にかやって来ていた春の訪れを喜んでいる。

Meaning of Tanka and Ryōkan's heart:
　Before I could even tell if spring had arrived, the fresh grass in the fields was beginning to sprout.

　Ryōkan rejoices at the arrival of spring as he hadn't noticed it.

32
> In the spring field,
> picking violets by hand
> I remembered my home
>
> 野に菫摘みて故郷(ふるさと)を思ひ出し
> *No ni Sumire　tsumite furusato　omoidashi*

元歌　春の野に咲ける菫を手に摘みて
　　　　吾が故郷を思ほゆるかな

Haru no no ni/ sakeru sumire wo/ te ni tsumite

waga furusato wo/ omowoyuru kana

歌意と良寛の心情：　春がやって来て野原一面に咲いている菫を手で摘み取っていると、幼い頃に故郷で草花を摘んでいたことを懐かしく思い出すよ。

年老いた良寛、菫を摘みながら故郷での日々を思い出している。

Meaning of Tanka and Ryōkan's heart:

　As spring comes and the fields are covered in blooming violets, I am reminded of my childhood home.

　Picking violets sparks a memory of his childhood for a now elderly Ryōkan.

33
> At the old temple
> I am alone today too
> picking Japanese star anises
>
> 樒摘み古寺に今日もひとり居り
> しきみ　　こじ
> *Shikimi tsuni   koji ni kyō mo   hitori wori*

元歌　古寺にひとりしをれば術をなみ
　　　　　　樒摘みつつ今日も暮らしぬ
　　　ふるでら　　　　　　　　　すべ

Hurudera ni/ hitorishi woreba/ sube wo nami

　　shikimi tsumi tsutsu/ kyō mo kurashinu

歌意と良寛の心情：　古寺にひとりでいると何もすることがなく、樒を摘んで今日も過ごしていたよ。
　（樒は常緑小高木。山地に自生し、墓地などに植えられている。春、黄白色の花をつける。葉と木皮は線香の材料に。秋、星形の果実を結ぶ。実は毒性あり。）
　　しきみ

Meaning of Tanka and Ryokan's heart:
　Being alone at the old temple, I had nothing to do, so I spent the day picking Japanese star anise.
　(Japanese star anise is an evergreen short tree that grows wild, and is often planted in graveyards. Yellowish-white flowers bloom on this tree in spring. The leaves and the bark are used as material for incense. It bears star-shaped fruit in autumn. The fruits are poisonous.)

34
> A single violet
> planted in my home
> may begin to bloom
>
> 宿に植ゆ　一本菫　咲き初むらん
> *Yado ni uyu　hitomoto sumire　saki somuran*

元歌　我が宿に一本植ゑし菫草
　　　　今は春べと咲き初めぬらむ

Waga yado ni/ hitomoto ueshi/ sumiregusa
　　　ima wa harube to/ saki somenuran

歌意と良寛の心情：　わたしの宿に一株の菫を植えたが、今は春になったと咲き初めているよ。

　良寛は晩年木村家（現 長岡市和島）の草庵で過ごした。その頃の歌。

Meaning of Tanka and Ryōkan's heart:
　I previously planted a single violet at my home, now that spring is here, it is beginning to bloom.

　This tanka might have been written from a hut where Ryōkan spent his later years and that was owned by the Kimura family (present day Wajima, Nagaoka City).

| 35 | In the spring breeze
gathering around a willow tree
and chatting with others

春風の柳に集ひ語り合ふ
Harukaze no　yanagi ni tsudoi　katari au |

元歌　春風の柳のもとに円居して
　　　　遊ぶ今日しは心のどけき

(まどゐ)

Harukaze no/ yanagi no motoni/ madoi shite
　　asobu kyō shi wa/ kokoro nodokeki

歌意と良寛の心情：　春のそよ風が吹く柳の下に円座して集まり、楽しく語り合う今日一日は心が安らぐことよ。
　「今日しは」…「し」は語調を整え、強意を表す。

村人たちと楽しく語り合うことが好きな良寛。

Meaning of Tanka and Ryōkan's heart:
　　We gathered under the willow trees in the spring breeze, sitting in a circle and chatting away, our hearts at peace.

Ryōkan enjoyed talking about different topics with the villagers.

36
> Pine and oak trees
> growing on the peaks
> enveloped in a spring haze
>
> 峯に立つ松や柏の春がすみ
> *Mine ni tatsu   matsu ya kashiwa no   harugasumi*

元歌　あしびきの峯の上(おえ)に立てる松柏
　　　　今は春べとうちかすみけり

Ashibikino/ onoe ni tateru/ matsu kashiwa
　　　ima wa harube to/ uchi kasumikeri

歌意と良寛の心情：　峯の上に立っている松や柏の木はいつも同じだが、今は春になったと、かすんで見えているよ。

　春がすみにかすんで見える周りの山々、良寛は雪国に春が来ていると実感。

Meaning of Tanka and Ryōkan's heart:
　The pine and oak trees growing on the peaks are always the same, but now they appear hazy, a signal that spring has come.

　Ryōkan might be feeling spring as he lives in the snow country and sees the mountain landscapes around him.

> 37　Talking together and
> getting drunk with sake
> spring is happy for us
>
> 語りあひ酒に酔ひたる春楽し
> 　*Katari ai　sake ni yoi taru　haru tanoshi*

元歌　さすたけの君と語りてうま酒に
　　　　あくまで酔へる春ぞ楽しき

Sasutakeno/ kimi to katarite/ umazake ni

akumade yoeru/ haru zo tanoshiki

歌意と良寛の心情：　永い冬も終わり、友（阿部定珍のこと）と語らいながらおいしいお酒を、心おきなく飲んで酔い祝う春は楽しいことよ。

（良寛の友定珍の阿部家は代々の造り酒屋である。）

お酒の好きな良寛、春の到来を友人定珍宅で酔う程に飲み、楽しんでいる。

Meaning of Tanka and Ryōkan's heart:
　Spring is a pleasant time for Ryōkan to get drunk from sake and chat with his friend Sadayoshi.
　(The Abe family, to which his friend Sadayoshi belonged, had operated a sake brewery for generations.)

Ryokan, who loved sake more than almost anything else, had a pleasant time on this spring day.

38
> I visited you
> with the picked blessings
> getting wet in snow melted water
>
> 雪解水濡れて摘み来るめぐみかな
> ゆきげみず
> *Yukigemizu　nurete tsumi kuru　megumi kana*

元歌　久方の雪解の水に濡れにつつ
　　　　　春のものとて摘みて来にけり

　　Hisakatano/ yukige no mizu ni/ nure ni tsutsu
　　　　haru no mono tote/ tsumi te kini keri

歌意と良寛の心情：　冷たい雪解け水に濡れながら、春の山菜を摘んで出かけて来たよ。

　雪残る塩入峠を越えて、途中山菜を摘みながら、与板の弟由之を訪れた良寛。
しおのり　　　　　　　　　　　　　　　　　　　　　ゆうし

Meaning of Tanka and Ryōkan's heart:
　While I was soaked in the cold meltwater from the snow, I was picking edible wild plants when I visited you.

　Ryōkan joyfully met his younger brother Yūshi visiting him at his home in Yoita (present day Yoita, Nagaoka City) picking wild plants on the way.

> 39　After Yamasakuras have now fallen,
> I want to bloom next
> the Japanese roses
>
> 山桜散りて咲きこせ山吹よ
> 　*Yamasakura　chirite saki kose　yamabuki yo*

元歌　あしびきの山の桜はうつろひぬ
　　　　次ぎて咲きこせ山吹の花

Ashibikino/ yama no sakura wa/ utsuroinu
　　tsugite saki kose/ yamabuki no hana

歌意と良寛の心情：　山桜の花は散ってしまった。山吹の花よ、続いて咲いて欲しいものだ。

初夏に咲く山吹の花が待ち遠しい良寛。

Meaning of Tanka and Ryōkan's heart:

　The mountain cherry blossoms have already fallen. I want Japanese roses to bloom next.

　Ryōkan was looking forward to Japanese roses blooming in the early summer.

40
> Japanese roses :
> a single petaled flower
> is most beautiful
>
> 山吹の一重(ひとへ)の花ぞ美しき
> *Yamabuki no   hitoe no hana zo   utsukushiki*

元歌　山吹の千重(ちへ)を八千重に重ぬとも
　　　　此(この)ひと花の一重にしかず

　　Yamabuki no/ chie wo yachie ni/ kasanu tomo
　　　kono hitohana no/ hitoe ni shikazu

歌意と良寛の心情：　幾重にも花びらを重ねた花よりも、山吹はそそとした一重の花ほど美しい。

　（山野に自生するものは一重で、八重の山吹は園芸品種である。）

良寛は山野に自生する一重の山吹に美を見出していた。

Meaning of Tanka and Ryōkan's heart:

　For Japanese roses, a simple, single petaled flower is more beautiful than a flower with many petals.

　(Japanese roses growing in the wild which grow in fields and mountains are all a single petaled variety, while the double petaled variety is a cultivar for gardening.)

Ryōkan found beauty in the single petaled, wild Japanese rose.

> 41 Becoming a hermit
> there is remaining life
> on the moon and blossoms
>
> 世捨て人なりて月花の余生かな
> *Yosutebito   narite gekka no   yosei kana*

元歌　世を棄て身を棄て閑者となりて
　　　　初めて月と花とに余生を送る

　　Yo wo sute/ mi wo sute/ kannja to narite
　　　　hajimete tsuki to/ hana to ni/ yosei wo okuru

歌意と良寛の心情：　浮き世を捨て、この身も捨てて閑者となりて、初めて月と花とを楽しむ余生が送られるよ。

世捨て人となり、自然を友とすることができた良寛。

Meaning of Tanka and Ryōkan's heart:
　　After becoming a hermit, I have abandoned this world and myself, and I spend the rest of my life enjoying gazing at the moon and flowers.

Ryōkan became a hermit and was able to make nature his friend.

42 I am satisfied
with my humble hut where
the moon and blossoms are as well

月も花もある草庵や満ちたりし
Tsuki mo hana mo   aru sōan ya   michitarishi

元歌   こと足らぬ身とは思わじ柴の戸に
　　　　　月も有りけり花もありけり

Koto taranu/ mi towa omowaji/ shiba no to ni
tsuki mo arikeri/ hana mo arikeri

歌意と良寛の心情:　住んでいる庵が柴の戸で粗末なものであっても、生活が満ち足らぬとは思わない。月や花があるのだから。

　自然の中での生活が好きな良寛、月を眺め、花に囲まれた生活に満足している。

Meaning of Tanka and Ryōkan's heart:

　Even though my simple hut is made of reed and brushwood, I don't feel unfulfilled because I can enjoy the moon and flowers.

Ryōkan enjoyed nature and felt joy looking at the moon and flowers.

> 43
>
> This world is like
> waving seaweeds growing
> in the inlet of Koshi in spring
>
> 世は越の春の浦生ふ藻のごとく
> *Yowa koshi no   haru no ura ou   mo no gotoku*

元歌　世間(よのなか)は越の浦わに生ふる藻の
　　　　かにもかくにも波のまにまに

Yononaka wa/ koshi no urawa ni/ ouru mo no
　　kanimo kakunimo/ nami no manimani

歌意と良寛の心情：　世の中は越後の海岸に生えている藻のように、とにかく波まかせに過ごすのがよい。

自然にまかせて生きて行くのがよいと達観している良寛。

Meaning of Tanka and Ryōkan's heart:

　In this world, it is better to live like the seaweed of the Koshi inlet that is carried by the waves.

　Ryōkan had the philosophical view that it is best to live in harmony with nature.

44　A change of clothes :
among deep mountains
the birds in spring yet singing

衣更へ深山（みやま）は春の鳥の鳴く
Koromogae　miyama wa haru no　tori no naku

元歌　夏衣たちてきぬれど深山（みやま）べは
　　　　いまだ春かも鶯の鳴く

Natsugoromo/ tachite kinuredo/ miyamabe wa
　　imada haru kamo/ uguisu no naku

歌意と良寛の心情：　夏の衣に替えてはみたが、山深い当地はまだ春のようで鶯が鳴いているよ。

里は初夏でも深山は鶯の鳴く春なのだ。

Meaning of Tanka and Ryōkan's heart:
　　Though I have changed into my summer clothes, it still feels like spring in the deep mountains with the bush warblers singing.
　　(June and October are the months for seasonal clothing changes in Japan.)

　　Although the villages in the mountain's foothills are now in summer, in the deep mountains the bush warblers are singing and it feels like spring.

> 45　Over Mount Kugami,
> little mountain cuckoos
> singing here and there
>
> 国上越え山時鳥をちこちに
> *Kugami goe　yamahototogisu　ochikochi ni*

元歌　あしびきの国上の山を越えくれば
　　　　山時鳥をちこちに鳴く

Ashibikino/ Kugami no yama wo/ koekure ba
　　　yamahototogisu/ ochikochi ni naku

歌意と良寛の心情：　国上の山を越えて来ると、山時鳥があちらこちらで鳴いていたよ。

　時鳥が好きな良寛、山道を歩きながらその鳴き声に耳を澄ませていた。

Meaning of Tanka and Ryōkan's heart:
　On the way over Mt.Kugami, I heard the songs of little mountain cuckoos singing here and there.

　Ryōkan, who likes little cuckoos, listened carefully to their songs while walking along the mountain pass.

46　Walking the pass around foothill
little cuckoos singing
and flying between trees

山辺道群れ鳴く子規(しき)の木の間飛ぶ
　　　　　　　（子規－時鳥の異名、明治以降に使用）
Yamabemichi　mure naku shiki no　konoma tobu

元歌　み山辺をたどりつつ来し郭公(ほととぎす)
　　　　　木の間たちくき鳴き羽振る見ゆ

Miyamabe wo/ tadoritsutsu kishi/ hototogisu
　　konoma tachikuki/ naki haburu miyu

歌意と良寛の心情：　夏草茂る山辺の道を歩いていると、時鳥が木の間をわき立つように鳴きながら羽ばたいて飛んでいるのがみられたよ。

良寛が出会ったのは時鳥の繁殖期の行動か。

Meaning of Tanka and Ryōkan's heart:
　　As I was walking along a mountain pass, I saw a flock of little cuckoos singing and flying between trees.

　　The scene Ryōkan encountered might be the behavior of little cuckoos during the breeding season.

> 47　Mount Kugami :
> now little cuckoos
> singing vigorously
>
> 国上山鳴く時鳥いま盛り
> 　Kugamiyama　naku hototogisu　ima sakari

元歌　あしびきの国上の山のほととぎす
　　　　今は盛りとふりはへて鳴く

Ashibikino/ kugami no yama no/ hototogisu
ima wa sakari to/ furihaete naku

歌意と良寛の心情：　国上山の時鳥は今が盛り（繁殖の時季）と、ことさらに鳴いているよ。

前歌（46）と同じ情景の中にいる良寛。

Meaning of Tanka and Ryōkan's heart:
　The little cuckoos living on Mt.Kugami are vigorously singing, as they are now in their prime (most likely breeding season).

This tanka describes the same scene as the former one (No.46).

> 48　Between trees
> a crescent moon
> is faintly seen
>
> 木の間より弓張の月ほのか見ゆ
> 　　*Konoma yori　yumihari no tsuki　honoka miyu*

元歌　おしなべて緑にかすむ木の間より
　　　　ほのかに見ゆる弓張の月

Oshinabete/ midori ni kasumu/ konoma yori
honoka ni miyuru/ yumihari no tsuki

歌意と良寛の心情：　一面にかすむような緑の木の間に、弓張の月がほんのりと見えるよ。

夕暮れの時、西の空にかかった弓張の月に心を惹かれた良寛。

Meaning of Tanka and Ryōkan's heart:
Between the hazy green trees, I can faintly see a crescent moon.

Ryōkan was moved by seeing the crescent moon setting in the western sky.

> 49　Mount Nodumi :
> in full bloom of deutzias
> I came here like dividing snow
>
> 野積山卯の花盛り雪を分け
> 　*Nodumiyama　unohana sakari　yuki wo wake*

元歌　卯の花の咲きのさかりは野積山
　　　　雪をわけゆく心地こそすれ

Unohana no/ saki no sakari wa/ nodumiyama
　yuki wo wakeyuku/ kokochi koso sure

歌意と良寛の心情：　卯の花の盛りに野積の山に行くと、雪をかきわけて行くような心地がするよ。

白い卯の花を降り積もった雪に見立て楽しんでいる良寛。

Meaning of Tanka and Ryōkan's heart:
　Coming to the Mt. Kugami where the deutzias are in full bloom, I feel as if I'm shoveling snow.

Ryōkan enjoys comparing the white deutzia flowers to snow.

> 50　By frogs croaking
> in the rice fields among hills,
> no good sleep alone
>
> 山田鳴く蛙にひとり寝ねむられず
> 　*Yamada naku　kawazu ni hitorine　nemurarezu*

元歌　あしびきの山田の原に蛙鳴く
　　　　ひとり寝る夜のい寝られなくに

　Ashibikino/ yamada no hara ni/ kawazu naku
　　　hitori neru yo no/ inerarenaku ni

歌意と良寛の心情：　山間(やまあい)の田に蛙が夜通し鳴いている。ひとりで寝ているとなかなか寝られないものだ。

　　一人寝の良寛の人恋しさの心情だ。

Meaning of Tanka and Ryōkan's heart:

　Frogs are croaking all night long in the rice fields among the hills. I couldn't sleep well alone.

　Ryōkan may have felt lonely in his life at night.

> 51　Some sunshine in rain
> going out and looking around,
> mountains all over deep green
>
> 雨晴れて出で見る四方の山青く
> *Ame hare te　idemiru yomo no　yama aoku*

元歌　ひさかたの雨の晴れ間に出でてみれば
　　　　青み渡りぬ四方の山々

Hisakatano/ ame no harema ni/ ide te mireba
aomi watarinu/ yomo no yamayama

歌意と良寛の心情：　あめの晴れ間に外に出て見ると、周りの山々は青み渡ってきているよ。

新緑だった山々は梅雨の間に、どんどん緑濃くなってゆく自然の力に感じ入る良寛。

Meaning of Tanka and Ryōkan's heart:
　When I went out of my hermitage on a clear day, I noticed all the mountains changing to a deep green.

　Ryōkan is deeply moved by the power of nature, seeing the green tree leaves progressively change from fresh to deeper green during the rainy season.

52
> People untainted
> are precious
> like the lotus flowers in morning
>
> 汚れなき人の尊さ朝の蓮
> *Yogore naki　hito no tōtosa　asa no hasu*

元歌　朝露にきほひて咲けるはちすばの
　　　　塵には染まぬ人のたふとさ

Asatsuyu ni/ kioite sakeru/ hachisuba no
　　chiri niwa shimanu/ hito no tōtosa

歌意と良寛の心情：　朝露の中競うように咲いている蓮の花のように、塵に染まらない人の心こそ尊いのだ。

　世の中の不正の横行を目にして、蓮の花にたとえ、汚れ無き人の尊さを説いている良寛。

Meaning of Tanka and Ryōkan's heart:
　Like the lotus flowers blooming in the morning dew, the heart of a person untainted by the dust of the world is truly precious.

　Seeing the rampant injustice in the world, Ryōkan compares it to a lotus flower and preaches about the preciousness of pure people.

> 53 The sound breezing through
> the bamboo grove of my home
> is clear
>
> 我が宿の竹吹く風の音清し
> *Waga yado no   take fuku kaze no   oto kiyoshi*

元歌　わが宿の竹の林をうち越して
　　　　　吹きくる風のおとの清さよ

Waga yado no/ take no hayashi wo/ uchi koshite
　　fukikuru kaze no/ oto no kiyosa yo

歌意と良寛の心情：　わたしの庵の竹林を越えて吹いて来る風の音はさわやかだ。

　自然に生きる良寛、竹林を吹き抜けて来る風の音にも心が動くのだ。

Meaning of Tanka and Ryōkan's heart:
　The sound of the breeze blowing through the bamboo grove of my hermitage is refreshing.

　Ryōkan lived in nature and was moved by the sound of wind.

54
> Rain and rain
> until the rice seedlings in mountain fields
> will be covered with rainy water
>
> 雨よ降れ山田の早苗かくるまで
> *Ame yo fure   yamada no sanae   kakuru made*

元歌　ひさかたの雨も降らなむあしびきの
　　　　山田のなへのかくるるまでに

Hisakatano/ amemo furanan/ ashibikino
　　　yamada no nae no/ kakururu made ni

歌意と良寛の心情：　山田の苗が水でかくれるまで、雨が降ってほしいよ。

良寛は常に農民に思いを寄せていた。

Meaning of Tanka and Ryōkan's heart:
　　I want it to rain until the rice seedlings in the fields among the hills are covered in water.

　　Ryōkan always loved farmers.

55　Looking around the sea
waving by the white south wind,
it merges into clouds

見わたせば白南風(しらはえ)の海雲にとけ
Miwataseba　shirahae no umi　kumo ni toke

元歌　白波の寄する渚を見わたせば
　　　　末は雲井に続く海原

Shiranami no/ yosuru nagisa wo/ miwataseba
sue wa kumoi ni/ tsuduku unabara

歌意と良寛の心情：　白波が打ち寄せる渚を見渡していると、遠くは雲と海原が続いて見えるよ。

空も海もつながっているように、人の世も広くつながっているのだとの良寛の心境。

Meaning of Tanka and Ryōkan's heart:
　Looking out over the shore being washed by white waves with the south wind blowing, the sea is melting into the clouds in the distance.

　Ryōkan felt that just as the sky and sea are connected, the human world is also widely connected.

182

56

Blossoms fell off :
no one called on me,
only bedstraws will be growing

花は散る問ふ人のなく八重葎
Hana wa chiru　tou hito no naku　yaemugura

元歌　花は散る問ふ人はなし今よりは
　　　　八重葎のみ這ひ茂るらん

Hana wa chiru/ tou hito wa nashi/ ima yoriwa
　　yaemugura nomi/ haishigeruran

歌意と良寛の心情：　桜の花の頃には訪ねて来てくれた人々も今はなく、八重葎が這い茂っているよ。

　花が終わると、訪ね来る人のいなくなった草庵で、ひとり淋しく思う良寛。

Meaning of Tanka and Ryōkan's heart:
　While cherry blossoms were blooming, many people visited me, but since the blossoms are now gone, no one calls on me. Around my hut only bedstraws are growing.

　Ryōkan is feeling lonely in his hermitage with no visitors once the cherry blossoms have fallen.

> 57　Summer grass
> growing thicker and thicker
> no one calls on my humble hut
>
> 夏草の茂れる我が宿人のなく
> 　*Natsukusa no　shigereru waga yado　hito no naku*

元歌　夏草の茂りに茂るわが宿は
　　　　かりにだにやも訪ふ人はなし

Natsukusa no/ shigeri ni shigeru/ waga yado wa
　　kari ni dani yamo/ tou hito wa nashi

歌意と良寛の心情：　夏草が茂りに茂っている私の草庵には、仮初めであっても訪れてくれる人はいないのだ。

夏の草庵には誰も訪ねて来ない良寛の寂しさ。

Meaning of Tanka and Ryōkan's heart:
　　At the moment, summer grass is growing thicker and thicker around my hermitage, no one has even called on me.

　　Ryōkan might feel lonely because no one has visited his humble hut in the summertime.

> 58　With dew in the morning and evening
> pinks begin to bloom
> in the field
>
> 朝夕の露に撫子野辺に咲き
> *Asayū no　tsuyu ni nadeshiko　nobe ni saki*

元歌　朝夕の露が情けの秋近み
　　　　野辺の撫子華咲きにけり

Asayū no/ tsuyu ga nasake no/ aki chikami
　　nobe no nadeshiko/ hana saki ni keri

歌意と良寛の心情：　秋も近づき、朝夕の冷え込みで露が降り、撫子の花が咲き出したよ。

草花の好きな良寛、撫子の花に移り行く季節を感じている。

Meaning of Tanka and Ryōkan's heart:

　　Autumn is approaching, the mornings and evenings are chilly, causing dew to fall, and the pink flowers have begun to bloom.

　　Ryōkan, who loved flowers, felt the changing seasons seeing pink flowers.

> 59　Under the clear sky
> Sado Island appears
> at the end of the sea
>
> 天高し海の果てなる佐渡が島
> 　Ten takashi　umi no hate naru　Sadogashima

元歌　天(あめ)も水もひとつに見ゆる海の上に
　　　　浮かび出でたる佐渡が島山

Ame mo mizu mo/ hitotsu ni miyuru/ umi no ue ni

ukabi ide taru/ sadogashima yama

歌意と良寛の心情：　空と海がひとつになって見える水平線上に、浮かぶように出ているのは佐渡が島の山々だよ。

　（良寛の母は佐渡市相川の生まれ。）

晴れた日に対岸から佐渡島を眺めるのが好きだった良寛。

Meaning of Tanka and Ryōkan's heart:

　Where the sea merges into the sky, the mountains of Sado Island appear to float on the horizon.

　(Ryōkan's mother was born in Aikawa, Sado city.)

　Ryōkan liked to look at Sado Island from the opposite shore on a clear day.

60
> Autumn in my humble hut :
> my mind is clear
> living day by day
>
> 庵の秋　その日暮らしも　心澄み
> *Io no aki　sonohigurashi mo　kokoro sumi*

元歌　詫びぬれど心は澄めり草の庵
　　　　その日その日を送るばかりに

Wabinuredo/ kokoro wa sumeri/ kusa no io
sonohi sonohi wo/ okuru bakari ni

歌意と良寛の心情：　草の庵での質素な暮らし、わびしさを覚えるも、心は澄み、その日その日を送っているのだよ。

貧しさの中にも、秋の空のように、心は澄みきっている良寛。

Meaning of Tanka and Ryōkan's heart:

I feel lonely living a simple life in my humble hut, but my mind is clear and I'm living day by day.

Ryōkan's mind is clear like the autumn sky, enjoying a simple life.

187

61
If fleas and lice could sing
my bosom would be
the autumn field

蚤虱 鳴かば懐 秋の原
Nomi shirami   nakaba futokoro   aki no hara

元歌　蚤虱音を立てて鳴く虫ならば
　　　　わが懐は武蔵野の原

Nomi shirami/ ne wo tatete naku/ mushi naraba
waga futokoro wa/ musashino no hara

歌意と良寛の心情：　蚤や虱が鳴く虫ならば、私の懐は秋の武蔵野の原のようだろう。

蚤や虱にも情けをかける良寛。

Meaning of Tanka and Ryōkan's heart:

　　If fleas and lice could sing, my heart would be like the Musashino plains in fall.

　　Ryōkan shows mercy to fleas and lice, too.

62

In my humble hut
a cricket begins to chirp
this evening

吾が庵にこほろぎ鳴き初むこの夕べ
Waga io ni   kōrogi naki somu   kono yūbe

元歌 この夕べ秋は来ぬらしわが門に
　　　つづれさせてふ虫の声する

Kono yūbe/ aki wa kinurashi/ waga kado ni
　　　tsuduresase chou/ mushi no koe suru

歌意と良寛の心情： 今宵は秋がやって来たようだ。私の住いの門のところで、こおろぎの鳴く音が聞こえ出したよ。

こおろぎの鳴く音に秋の気配を感じた良寛。

Meaning of Tanka and Ryōkan's heart:

　It seems that autumn has arrived tonight, since I can hear a cricket chirping at the gate of my home.

　Ryōkan felt the coming of fall by a cricket's chirping.

> 63 Like swaying sleeves
> the first ears of pampas grass
> beckon people
>
> 初尾花袖ふるごとく人招く
> *Hatsuobana   sode furu gotoku   hito maneku*

元歌　秋されば一群 薄 初尾花
　　　　　　（ひとむらすすき）
　　　人を招くよ袖とみゆらん

　　Aki sareba/ hitomura susuki/ hatsuobana
　　　　hito wo manekuyo/ sode to miyuran

歌意と良寛の心情：　秋がやって来て一群のすすきに尾花が咲き、人を招くよう袖を振っているかのように見えるよ。

風に揺れる初尾花、良寛には人を招くように思われた。

Meaning of Tanka and Ryōkan's heart:
　　As it has been autumn, the first ears of Japanese pampas grass are growing, and they seem to be waving sleeves inviting people.

　　In a breeze, Ryōkan thinks the first pampas grass ears appear to be beckoning people.

> 64
> In front of my gate
> the evening breeze over the rice leaves
> is sorrowful somehow
>
> わが門の稲葉の夕風うら哀し
> *Waga kado no　inaba no yūkaze　uraganashi*

元歌　何となくうら哀しきはわが門の
　　　　　稲葉そよげる秋の夕風

Nantonaku/ uraganashiki wa/ waga kado no
　　inaba soyogeru/ aki no yūkaze

歌意と良寛の心情：　何となく心哀しく思われることは、わたしの門の前の稲田の葉をそよそよとなびかせて吹いて来る秋の夕風であるよ。

秋の実りを前にして稲田を渡るそよ風に、なぜか心哀しさを覚える良寛。

Meaning of Tanka and Ryōkan's heart:
　　The autumn evening breeze blowing somehow makes me feel sad as it gently rustles the leaves in the rice field in front of my gate.

　　For some reason, Ryōkan felt sorrow in the breeze in the evening over the rice field before the harvest.

65　The sparkling dew on pampas grass
　　growing in my yard
　　I look at it without being tired

　　宿に生ふ薄の白露飽かず見ゆ
　　　Yado ni ou　susuki no shiratsuyu　akazu miyu

元歌　行き返り見れども飽かず我が宿の
　　　　薄が上に置ける白露

Yuki kaeri/ miredomo akazu/ waga yado no
susuki ga ue ni/ okeru shiratsuyu

歌意と良寛の心情：　宿に生えている薄の葉に、こぼれそうでこぼれず乗っている光る白露、行き来に見ても飽きることはないよ。

何時零(こぼ)れ落ちるか分からない薄の葉の白露、晩年の良寛の心情だ。

Meaning of Tanka and Ryōkan's heart:
　　I never tire of looking at the sparkling dew on the pampas grass leaves as I pass by.

　　Ryōkan's heart later in his life was that he thought himself similar to the dew on the leaves of pampas grass, potentially dropping at any moment.

66
> Patrinias blooming in the morning dew :
> no person I would like
> to pick them for
>
> 摘み贈る人なき露の女郎花
> *Tsumi okuru   hito naki tsuyu no   ominaeshi*

元歌　白露に乱れて咲ける女郎花
　　　　摘みて贈らむその人なしに

Shiratsuyu ni/ midarete sakeru/ ominaeshi
　　tsumite okuran/ sonohito nashi ni

歌意と良寛の心情：　白く光って見える露にぬれ、乱れて咲いている女郎花、その黄花を摘んで贈りたいが、そのような人がいないのだ。

孤独な良寛の心境。

Meaning of Tanka and Ryōkan's heart:
　The yellow patrinia flowers are blooming in riotous numbers, wet with sparkling dew.
　I would like to pick some of them, but I have no one to share them with.

This tanka poem shows Ryōkan's lonely state of mind.

| 67 | Coming to see patrinias,
the morning mist
is covering them

我見に来し朝霧隠す女郎花
Ware minikishi　asagiri kakusu　ominaeshi |

元歌　ことさらに我が見に来れば朝霧に
　　　　立ちかくしけり女郎花のはな

Kotosarani/ waga mini kureba/ asagiri ni
　　　tachikakushikeri/ ominaeshi no hana

歌意と良寛の心情：　わざわざ私が見に来たのに、女郎花の花は朝霧に隠されていたよ。

自然の中で草花を見ることが好きだった良寛。

Meaning of Tanka and Ryōkan's heart:
　Even though I have come all the way to see the yellow patrinia flowers, they were hidden by the morning mist.

Ryōkan enjoyed looking at flowers in fields in nature.

68
> A monk alone
> hearing insect song and
> looking at a distant village in fog
>
> 僧ひとり虫音聞き見る霧の里
> *Sō hitori　mushine kiki miru　kiri no sato*

元歌　秋の夕(ゆふべ)虫音を聞きに僧ひとり
　　　遠方(をちかた)里は霧に埋(うず)まる

Aki no yūbe/ mushine wo kiki ni/ sou hitori
ochikata sato wa/ kiri ni uzumaru

歌意と良寛の心情：　秋の夕暮れに、ひとりの僧が虫の音を聞きながら立っている。遠くに見える村里は霧に埋まっているようだ。

僧ひとりは良寛自身であろう。

Meaning of Tanka and Ryōkan's heart:
　On an autumn evening, a monk stands listening to the sounds of insects. In the distance, a village seems to be shrouded in mist.

The standing monk might be Ryōkan himself.

> 69 Coming on the mountain pass,
> patrinias grow as if standing
> getting wet with morning mist
>
> 山路来て朝霧ぬれ立つ女郎花
> *Yamaji kite   asagiri nuretatsu   ominaeshi*

元歌　秋山をわが越えくれば女郎花
　　　　あしたの霧にぬれつつ立てり

Akiyama wo/ waga koekureba/ ominaeshi
ashita no kiri ni/ nuretsutsu tateri

歌意と良寛の心情：　秋の山を我一人で越えて来ると、女郎花が朝の霧にぬれて立っているよ。

朝霧の立ち込める山路、良寛お出かけの途中での光景。

Meaning of Tankaand Ryōkan's heart:

　　As I cross a mountain pass in autumn alone, patrinias stand getting wet with the morning mist.

　　On his way out, Ryōkan, who loved flowers in nature, might be glad to find the yellow patrinia flowers standing in the morning mist.

70
> To whom will I give
> a thoroughwort blooming
> in glistened dew?
>
> 誰に贈らう白露に咲く藤ばかま
> *Tare ni okurou   shiratsuyu ni saku   fujibakama*

元歌　白露に競(きほ)て咲ける藤ばかま
　　　　摘みて贈らん其の人や誰

Shiratsuyu ni/ kiōte sakeru/ fujibakama
　　tsumite okuran/ sono hito ya tare

歌意と良寛の心情：　朝の光るような露に競うように咲いている藤袴を、摘んで贈ろうと思うが、誰ともまだ決めていないのだ。

　露に濡れ咲いている藤袴、摘んではみたものの、誰に贈ろうか戸惑っている良寛。

Meaning of Tanka and Ryōkan's heart:
　The thoroughworts bloom in competition with the glistened morning dew. I want to give them to someone, but I haven't decided yet.

　Ryōkan might be confused because he hasn't decided a person to whom he wanted to give the thoroughworts that he was picking.

| 71 | Dew like a bead
on the leaves in a field
disappeared I will get it

野の草の葉の露の玉取らば消え
No no kusa no　ha no tsuyu no tama　toraba kie |

元歌　秋の野の草葉の露を玉と見て
　　　　　取らむとすればかつ消えにけり

Aki no no no/ kusaba no tsuyu wo/ tama to mite
toran to sureba/ katsu kienikeri

歌意と良寛の心情：　秋の野で草葉にたまる朝露を玉と思って手で取ろうとすると、すぐにくずれて消えてしまうよ。

草の露を現世に見立てている良寛。

Meaning of Tanka and Ryōkan's heart:
　　As soon as I tried to pick up dew like a bead on the leaves in a field, it quickly disappeared.

Ryōkan regarded the world as dew on a leaf.

72
> Singing crickets
> disturbed
> my sleeping alone
>
> こほろぎの鳴くにひとり寝さまたげり
> *Kōrogi no   nakuni hitorine   samatageri*

元歌　いとどしく鳴くものにかもきりぎりす
　　　　　ひとり寝る夜のい寝られなくに

Itodoshiku/ nakumono ni kamo/ kirigirisu
hitori neru yo no/ inerarenaku ni

歌意と良寛の心情：　こおろぎの鳴く音がはなはだしいので、ひとりで寝る夜は寝られないものですよ。

人恋しい良寛には、ひとり寝は淋しいのである。

Meaning of Tanka and Ryōkan's heart:
　　The sound of the crickets chirping is so loud that I can't sleep at night when I sleep alone.

　　Ryōkan felt lonely sleeping all by himself.

73　When fall will arrive,
　　call on my humble hut
　　hearing the howl of stags

　　秋来(く)らば鹿の音(ね)聞きつ我が宿へ
　　Aki kuraba　shika no ne kikitsu　waga yado e

元歌　秋さらば訪ねて来ませ我宿を
　　　　　尾の上(え)の鹿の声聞きがてら

Aki saraba/ tazunete kimase/ waga yado wo
onoe no shika no/ koe kiki gatera

歌意と良寛の心情：　秋が来たならば我が草庵を訪ねて来なさいよ。峰で鳴いている雄鹿の声を聞きながら。

「さらば」は「然(さ)らば」…それならば、それでは

人の訪れが待ち遠しい良寛。

Meaning of Tanka and Ryōkan's heart:

When fall comes, please visit my humble hut, listening to the stags howling on the mountain peak.

Ryōkan could hardly wait for people to visit him.

74
> Coming somehow
> I am captivated
> by flowers of the field
>
> **なにげなく我来し花野心打つ**
> *Nanigenaku   ware kishi hanano   kokoro utsu*

元歌 等閑に我来しものを秋の野の
　　　　　花に心を尽くしつるかも

（なほざり）

Naozari ni/ ware koshi mono wo/ aki no no no

hana ni kokoro wo/ tsukushitsuru kamo

歌意と良寛の心情： 何となくやって来た秋の野の草花に、すっかり心を奪われてしっまたことよ。

野辺に咲いている草花をも愛する良寛の心情。

Meaning of Tanka and Ryōkan's heart:

I was completely captivated by the autumn flowers blooming on the field by chance.

Ryōkan showed his loving heart regarding the flowers of the field.

75 | At the inn dropping in
for begging rice
bush clovers in full bloom.

托鉢に寄る宿の萩盛りなり
Takuhatsu ni　yoru yado no hagi　sakari nari

元歌　飯乞ふと我が来にければこの宿の
　　　　　　萩の盛りに会ひにけるかも

Iikou to/ waga kinikere ba/ kono yado no
hagi no sakari ni/ ainikeru kamo

歌意と良寛の心情：　托鉢に回りながら寄って泊まったりもする宿に来てみると、庭に丁度盛りとなっている萩に出会えたことよ。

盛りの萩を見るのを楽しみにしている良寛。

Meaning of Tanka and Ryōkan's heart:

　　At the garden of the inn where I was begging for rice, I can see bush clovers in full bloom.

　　It was pleasant for Ryōkan to see bush clovers in full bloom.

76
> Red and yellow leaves in fall
> and little cuckoos in summer,
> I can't forget them
>
> **秋紅葉夏時鳥忘られじ**
> *Aki momiji   natsu hototogisu   wasurareji*

元歌　　**露霜の秋の紅葉と時鳥**
　　　　　　いつの世にかは我が忘れめや

　　　　Tsuyushimono/ aki no momiji to/ hototogisu
　　　　　　itsu no yonika wa/ waga wasuremeya

　　　　露霜の（tuyushimono）－「秋（aki-autumn）」にかかる掛る枕詞。

歌意と良寛の心情：　　日ごと深み行く紅葉の美しさと、夏の時鳥の鳴き声は、何時になっても私は忘れることはない。

移り変る季節に自然への深い思いを持つ良寛。

Meaning of Tanka and Ryōkan's heart:
　　I will never forget the beauty of the changing colored leaves in fall, nor the song of little cuckoos in summer.

Ryōkan had deep feelings for nature and the changing seasons.

> 77
>
> Breaking hagi and pampas grass
> with my hands
> I soaked them into my sleeves
>
> 萩すすき　手折りて衣手　染(し)みこませ
> *Hagi susuki　taorite koromode　shimikomase*

元歌　この岡の秋萩すすき手折りてむ
　　　　我が衣手に染まば染むとも

　　Konooka no/ aki hagi susuki/ taoriten
　　　　waga koromode ni/ shimaba shimutomo

歌意と良寛の心情：　この岡に生えている秋の萩の花やすすきを手でおり、衣の袖に花の香や色を染みるだけ染みこませようよ。

秋の衣更えの一時を楽しんでいる良寛。

Meaning of Tanka and Ryōkan's heart:

　　I picked the autumn hagi (bush clover) and pampas grass growing on this hill, and let the scent soak my sleeves.

　　Ryōkan is enjoying the moment of changing into autumn clothing.

78
> It's lonesome :
> songs of insects
> and flowers in a field
>
> 淋しさや虫の鳴く音に野辺の花
> *Sabishisaya   mushi no nakune ni   nobe no hana*

元歌　いつはとは時はあれども淋しさは
　　　　虫の鳴く音に野辺の草花

Itsuwatowa/ toki wa aredomo/ sabishisa wa

mushi no nakune ni/ nobe no hana

歌意と良寛の心情：　いつと言うのではないが、秋は虫の鳴く音を聞き、野の草花を見ていると淋しいものだよ。

　良寛はこの句と次の句（79）で、暮れて行く秋を虫や草花に思いを寄せて、自身の心の中を詠んでいる。

Meaning of Tanka and Ryōkan's heart:
　I can't explain why, but in the fall, listening to the sounds of insects chirping and looking at flowers in the field is a lonely experience.

　In this and Ryōkan's next tanka poems (79), he might be expressing his thoughts on fall drawing to a close.

79　The night is poignant :
the songs of insects
and many flowers wildly blooming

虫の音に乱れ咲く花夜はあはれ
Mushi no ne ni　midare sakuhana　yo wa aware

元歌　あはれさはいつはあれども秋の夜は
　　　　虫の鳴く音に八千草の花

Awaresa wa/ itsuwaare domo/ aki no yo wa
　　mushi no naku ne ni/ yachigusa no hana

歌意と良寛の心情：　自然の中ではしみじみとした哀感は何時の世でもあるものだが、深み行く秋の夜の虫の音や、野に乱れ咲く草花には心が動かされるよ。

　冬が近づくにつれ、姿を消す虫たちや野の草花に、ものの哀れを覚える良寛。

Meaning of Tanka and Ryōkan's heart:
　Because I always have a deep devotion to nature, the sounds of insect's songs on a deepening autumn night and wildly blooming flowers move my heart.

　Ryōkan felt profound sadness at the disappearance of insects and wild flowers as winter approached.

> 80 Dew on the pass and cold :
> would you like one more cup of sake
> before leaving here?
>
> **山路露寒し立ち酒いかがせむ**
> *Yamaji tsuyu   samushi tachizake   ikagasemu*

元歌　露は置きぬ山路は寒し立ち酒を
　　　　食（を）して帰らばけだしいかがあらむ

Tsuyu wa okinu/ yamaji wa samushi/ tachizake wo
　　　oshite kaeraba/ kedashi ikagaaran

歌意と良寛の心情：　夜露が降りている山道は寒い。お立ち酒を飲んで、元気をつけて帰られたらどうでしょう。

　人恋しい良寛、訪ねて来てくれた友をもう少し引き留めたいのだ。

Meaning of Tanka and Ryōkan's heart:
　The mountain pass is cold with night dew falling. Would you like to drink one more cup of sake before leaving?

　Ryōkan wanted to keep a visitor a little longer because he's a loving person.

81
> Cold-heartedly
> I came back leaving
> pale colored leaves
>
> 無情にも見捨て帰れり薄紅葉
> *Mujou nimo   misute kaereri   usumomiji*

元歌　山奥に見捨てて帰る薄紅葉
　　　　　我れを思はん浅き心と

Yamaoku ni/ misutete kaeru/ usumomiji
　　　ware wo omowan/ asaki kokoro to

歌意と良寛の心情：　奥深い山に色づき始めたうすき紅葉に、何の関心も持たずに帰った私を薄情な奴と思っているだろうよ。

　まだ紅葉の始まりの木々に関心を持たなかった自身に後悔している良寛。

Meaning of Tanka and Ryōkan's heart:
　I was maybe thought cold-hearted for returning home without paying attention to the pale autumn leaves in the deep mountains.

　Ryōkan regrets coldly ignoring the pale colored leaves on the mountain trees.

82　The songs of insects decreased :
the wind has become colder
night after night

虫音減る夜ごとの風の寒さ増し
Mushine heru　yogoto no kaze no　samusa mashi

元歌　虫の音も残り少なになりにけり
　　　　夜な夜な風の寒くしなれば

Mushi no ne mo/ nokori sukunani/ narinikeri
　　yonayona kaze no/ samukushi nareba

歌意と良寛の心情：　あれだけ賑やかだった秋の虫の音も、夜ごとに吹く風の寒さが増して、残り少なくなったよ。

　深み行く秋、虫の音に託して人生の悲哀さを感じている良寛。(84)の歌も同じ心境であろう。

Meaning of Tanka and Ryōkan's heart:
　The sounds of insects in the autumn were so lively, but are now dwindling as the winds grow colder night after night.

　In late fall, Ryōkan expresses his sorrow of life through the dwindling sounds of insects.
　Tanka poem No.84 is thought to express the same sentiments.

> 83 It may be good to rain :
> since we could together look at
> chrysanthemums in full bloom
>
> 菊さかりあひみて後の雨もよし
> *Kiku sakari   aimite nochi no   ame mo yoshi*

元歌   かみなづきしぐれふるともよしゑやし
　　　　　菊のさかりをあひみてのちは

Kaminaduki/ shigure furu tomo/ yoshieyashi
kiku no sakari wo/ aimite nochi wa

歌意と良寛の心情：　十月末の阿部定珍のお庭。盛りの菊の花を見れたので、もう何時時雨が降っても、思い残すことはないよ。

親友（定珍）と一緒に菊の盛りを見れた良寛の喜び。

Meaning of Tanka and Ryōkan's heart:
　At the end of October (using the old calendar) in the Abe's garden: I was happy to have enjoyed seeing full bloom chrysanthemums together with my friend Sadayoshi, so even though it rained, I have no regrets.

　Ryōkan might feel pleasure seeing the chrysanthemums together with his close friend Sadayoshi Abe.

　この短歌は阿部定珍の歌で、良寛歌集に誤って収められたものとされている。
　This tanka poem is thought to be one of Sadayoshi Abe's, mistakenly recorded in Ryōkan's book of poems.

84 Every night the wind becomes colder
in the field where bell crickets
remain chirping

夜々の風寒さ増す野に鈴虫や
Yoyo no kaze   samusa masu no ni   suzumushi ya

元歌　秋風の夜ごとに寒くなるなべに
　　　　枯野に残る鈴虫の声

Akikaze no/ yogoto ni samuku/ narunabeni
　　kareno ni nokoru/ suzumushi no koe

歌意と良寛の心情：　秋が深まるにつれ、風も夜ごとに寒くなってきた。しだいに草木も枯れてゆくなか、鈴虫のか弱い鳴き声が聞こえて来るよ。

Meaning of Tanka and Ryōkan's heart:
　　As the fall deepens, the wind has become colder every night. Only bell crickets remain chirping within the dying field. As the fields wither, only the weak chirps of the bell crickets can be heard.

> 85
>
> The mountain wind
> scatters occasionally
> even the non colored maple leaves
>
> 色づかぬ黄葉(もみじば)散らす山の風
>
> *Irodukanu　momijiba chirasu　yama no kaze*

元歌　山風は時し知らねば黄葉(もみじば)の
　　　　色づかぬ間を何か頼まむ

Yamakaze wa/ tokishi shiraneba/ momijiba no
irodukanu ma wo/ nanika tanoman

歌意と良寛の心情：　山の風は時節を考えずに吹くので、黄葉がまだ色づかない間は散らさないといえようか。

中川都良(とりょう)（与板の俳人、良寛の父以南の義弟）の訃報に接し詠んだ歌。良寛は義伯父都良の訃報に、もう少し生きてほしいと願った。

Meaning of Tanka and Ryōkan's heart:

　The mountain wind blows without regard for the seasons, so even maple leaves that are not yet colored may be scattered by it.

　Ryōkan wrote this poem when he heard the news of his uncle Toryō's death (Toryō Nakagawa, brother-in-law of Ryōkan's father Inan, a haiku poet who lived in Yoita). Ryōkan wanted his uncle Toryō to live a little longer.

> 86　Autumn has advanced :
> I am lonely indeed
> for the howl of stags
>
> 行く秋やほとほと恋し小牡鹿の声
> 　　*Yukuaki ya　hotohoto koishi　saoshika no koe*

元歌　秋もやや残り少なくなりぬれば
　　　　ほとほと恋し小牡鹿の声

Aki mo yaya/ nokori sukunaku/ narinureba
hotohoto koishi/ saoshika no koe

歌意と良寛の心情：　秋もだんだん残り少なくなってくると、牡鹿の鳴く声が本当に恋しくなってくるよ。
　「小牡鹿」…「小」は接頭語

暮れようとしている秋、淋しさが募って行く良寛。

Meaning of Tanka and Ryōkan's heart:
　　As autumn gradually comes to an end, I truly begin to miss the howl of stags.

　　In the advancing autumn, Ryōkan felt increasingly lonely.

87 Autumn has advanced :
let's go back
to my hut

秋深しいざ帰りなむ我が庵(いお)へ
Aki fukashi   iza kaerinan   waga io e

元歌　秋もややうら寂しくぞなりにけり
　　　　いざ帰りなむ草の庵(いほり)に

Aki mo yaya/ urasabishiku zo/ narinikeri

iza kaerinan/ kusa no iori ni

歌意と良寛の心情：　秋もしだいに深まり、なんとなく寂しくなってきた。さあ帰るとしよう我が庵へ。

陶淵明の「帰去来辞」を思い浮かべて詠んだもの。

Meaning of Tanka and Ryōkan's heart:

As the fall has gradually advanced, for some reason I feel lonely. Let's go back to my hut.

Ryōkan must have written this tanka poem as a homage to "Gui-qu-lai ci" by Tao Yuan-ming (365-427 AD).

> 88　If you called on me before 10 days ago,
> I could show you
> the colored leaves in mountains
>
> 十日前来たれば見せし山紅葉
> 　　*Tōka mae　kitareba miseshi　yamamomiji*

元歌　十日まり早くありせばあしびきの
　　　　　　山の紅葉を見せましものを

　　　　Tōka mari/ hayaku ariseba/ ashibikino
　　　　　　yama no momiji wo/ misemashi monowo

歌意と良寛の心情：　十日あまり早く訪れてくれたならば、山の盛りの紅葉をお見せできたのに。

五合庵の周りの山々の紅葉は素晴らしかったのだ。

Meaning of Tanka and Ryōkan's heart:
　　If you had come about 10 days ago, I could have shown you red and yellow leaves on the mountain.

　　The colored leaves of the mountains surrounding Gogōan were magnificent.

> 89 No songs of insects,
> it becomes cold
> with showers in late autumn
>
> 虫音絶え時雨れる秋の暮寒し
> *Mushine tae   shigureru aki no   kure samushi*

元歌　肌寒み秋も暮ぬと思ふかな
　　　　虫の音も離る時雨する夜は

(はだざむ)
(か)

Hadasamumi/ aki mo kurenu to/ omou kana
　　mushi no ne mo karu/ shigure suru yo wa

歌意と良寛の心情：　秋も深まり、虫の音も絶え、時雨れる夜は肌寒さが一段と身に染みて来るよ。

深まり行く秋、寒さがだんだんと身に染みて来た良寛。

Meaning of Tanka and Ryōkan's heart:
　　As autumn deepens, the sounds of insects gradually disappear and, I keenly feel the chill of nights with light rain.

Ryōkan might have felt much colder with advancing autumn.

90　Lonesome :
the colored leaves in the backs
had been scattered over

峰々の紅葉散りはてうらさびし
Minemine no　momiji chirihate　urasabishi

元歌　遠近(をちこち)の山の紅葉(もみぢ)ば散り過ぎて
　　　　うらさびしくぞ成りにけらしも

Ochikochi no/ yama no momijiba/ chirisugite
　　urasabishiku zo/ nari ni kerashimo

歌意と良寛の心情：　国上山の峰々を紅く染めていた紅葉もすっかり散り、なんとなく寂しい庵での暮らしになってしまったよ。

　紅葉も散り果て、秋も終わり、なんとなく寂しい暮らしとなった良寛。

Meaning of Tanka and Ryōkan's heart:
　The red and yellow leaves that dyed all sides of Mt.Kugami have scattered, so I now find myself living in a lonely hut.

　Ryōkan might feel melancholy after the falling of the autumn leaves.

91　The sounds of falling leaves like showers:
this morning I hear the rainy ones
in my humble hut of the village

木の葉時雨今朝は雨音里の庵
　Konohashigure　kesa wa amaoto　sato no io

元歌　はらはらと降るは木の葉の時雨にて
　　　　雨を今朝聞く山里の庵

Harahara to/ furu wa konoha no/ shigure nite
　　ame wo kesa kiku/ yamazato no io

歌意と良寛の心情：　国上山の庵にいると、風が吹くと枯れ葉が時雨のように降ってくる。今朝は雨音も混じって聞かれたよ。

秋から冬へと進んでゆく越後の自然に、寂しさを感じている良寛。

Meaning of Tanka and Ryōkan's heart:
　In my humble hut at Mt.Kugami, the wind blew, and the dead leaves fell like a light rain. This morning, I could hear the sounds of rain together with thc falling leaves.

　Ryōkan feels lonely as the nature of Echigo changes from fall to winter.

92
> As it has been raining,
> the colored leaves in the peaks
> had been all scattered
>
> 降り続く雨に紅葉の散り果てり
> *Furitsuduku   ame ni momiji no   chiri hateri*

元歌　久方の時雨の雨の間なく降れば
　　　　峯の紅葉は散りすぎにけり

Hisakatano/ shigure no ame no/ manaku fureba
　　mine no momiji wa/ chirisuginikeri

歌意と良寛の心情：　晴れ間なく降り続く時雨に、峰々の紅葉はすっかり散り果ててしまったよ。

　冬支度の出来上がった山々に、良寛は寂しさと春への期待を持ったのでは。

Meaning of Tanka and Ryōkan's heart:
　Due to the late autumn relentless drizzle, the colored leaves in the peaks have all been scattered.

　The peaks around Ryōkan's hut seem prepared for winter as all the dead leaves had already fallen. He might have felt lonely and looking forward to spring's arrival.

93　Colored leaves fall always :
for people
aging too

紅葉散る人とて同じ老いのあり
Momiji chiru　hito tote onaji　oi no ari

元歌　惜しめども盛りは過ぎぬ待たなくに
　　　　尋(と)めくるものは老いにぞありける

Oshimedomo/ sakari wa suginu/ matanaku ni
tomekuru mono wa/ oi nizo arikeru

歌意と良寛の心情：　紅葉も盛りが過ぎてしまうと冬がやって来るように、人も同じく老いがやって来る。待ってはくれないのだ。

　良寛は紅葉にたとえて、過ぎて行く人の世の侘しさ、老いの寂しさを詠んでいる。

Meaning of Tanka and Ryōkan's heart:
　　Just as winter comes after the prime of colored leaves in autumn, old age comes to people. It waits for no one.

　　Ryōkan compares the colored leaves to loneliness and old age.

94
With the water
dripping down from rocks
may I survive in this winter

岩垂るる水を命に冬しのぎ
Iwa taruru　mizu wo inochi ni　fuyu shinogi

元歌　岩が根にしたたる水を命にて
　　　　　今年の冬もしのぎつるかも

Iwa ga ne ni/ shitataru mizu wo/ inochi nite
　　　kotoshi no fuyu mo/ shinogi tsuru kamo

歌意と良寛の心情：　大きな岩から滴り落ちる水を命の支えとして、今年の厳しい冬も乗り越えてゆくことよ。
（この短歌は阿部定珍に万葉集拝借の依頼の書状につけて送られたもの）

「石走る垂水の上のさわらびの萌え出づる春になりにけるかも」
（志貴皇子・万葉集）を思い浮かべ、春が待ち遠しい良寛。

Meaning of Tanka and Ryōkan's heart:
　The water dripping down from these rocks will sustain me through this harsh winter.

　　Remembering a tanka poem in *Manyōshū*
　　　　Maybe spring
　　　　where ferns sprout
　　　　on the water dripping field
　　　　(composer: Shikinomiko),
　　Ryōkan wrote this poem looking forward to spring.
　　(This tanka was sent for Sadayoshi Abe with a letter requesting to borrow the *Manyōshū*.)

95 An early winter rain :
I can't go out to the village
begging for rice today too

時雨(しぐ)るるや飯乞(いひこ)ふ里に今日も出ず
Shigururuya　ii kou sato ni　kyō mo dezu

元歌　飯乞ふと里にも出(い)でずこの頃は
　　　　時雨の雨の間なくし降れば

Ii kou to/ sato nimo idezu/ konogoro wa
　　shigure no ame no/ manakushi fure ba

歌意と良寛の心情：　この頃冷たい時雨の雨が止むこともなく降るので、村里に托鉢に行こうにも、つい足が遠のいてしまうよ。

冬に備えての托鉢に出かけられないで困っている良寛。

Meaning of Tanka and Ryōkan's heart:

　　During these early winter days, it has been raining all day, so I have not gone out to the villages to beg for rice and other foods.

　　Ryōkan might be troubled by rain in early winter, unable to make preparations for winter proper.

96 Running water can be retained,
    but the passing time
    can't be checked

    流れは堰(せ)き止めても月日止められず
    Nagare wa   sekitome temo   tsukihi tomerarezu

元歌　行く水は堰きとどめてもありぬべし
　　　　　過ぎし月日のまた返るとは

Yukumizu wa/ sekitodome temo/ arinu beshi
　　sugishi tsukihi no/ mata kaeru towa

歌意と良寛の心情：　流れる水は堰き止めることはできても、過ぎた月日は取り戻すことはできない。

老いは止めることはできないのだと悟る良寛。

Meaning of Tanka and Ryōkan's heart:
　　Running water can be dammed, but the time that has passed is gone forever.

　　Ryōkan realized that aging couldn't be stopped.

97 Setting a checkpoint,
I would like to stop
the years of aging

関据ゑて老いの年月通らせじ
Seki suete   oi no toshitsuki   tōraseji

元歌　年月の来むと知りせばたまほこの
　　　　　道の巷（ちまた）に関据ゑましを

Toshitsuki no/ komu to shiriseba/ tamahokono
michi no chimata ni/ seki suemashiwo

たまほこの（tamahokono）－「道（michi-road）」にかかる掛る枕詞。

歌意と良寛の心情：　老いを連れて年月がやって来るのが、目に見えてわかるものならば、分かれ道に関所を設けて通さないようにしたいものだ。

老いに抵抗しようとする良寛。

Meaning of Tanka and Ryōkan's heart:
　　If I could foresee the passage of time and old age, I would set a checkpoint on the fork of life.

　　Ryōkan resisted getting old.

98
> Last and this year :
> aging is only accumulated
> every year
>
> 去年今年老いの年月つもりゆく
> <ruby>こぞことし</ruby>
> *Kozokotoshi　oi no toshituki　tsumori yuku*

元歌　年月は行きかもするに老いらくの
　　　　来れば行かずに何つもるらむ

Toshitsuki wa/ yuki kamo suru ni/ oiraku no
　　kure ba yukazu ni/ nani tsumoru ran

歌意と良寛の心情：　年月は知らぬ間に過ぎて行くが、老いはやって来るとどこにも行かず、積もって行くのだ。

老いを悟ってはいてもやはり気になる良寛。

Meaning of Tanka and Ryōkan's heart:

　Years pass by without us noticing, but when we reach old age, it doesn't go anywhere and keeps accumulating.

　Even though Ryōkan knows he is getting old, he is uneasy about aging.

> 99 Staying in my hut during winter,
> no traces of coming and going
> all season long
>
> 冬ごもり宿に行き来の跡もなし
> *Fuyugomori   yado ni yukiki no   ato mo nashi*

元歌   わが宿は越の白山(しろやま)冬ごもり
　　　　行き来の人の跡かたもなし

Waga yado wa/ koshi no shiroyama/ fuyugomori

yukiki no hito no/ atokata mo nashi

歌意と良寛の心情:　私の草庵も越後の雪に覆われ、冬ごもりに入り、行き来する人もなく、足跡も見られないよ。

　雪のため訪れる人のいない庵に、一人で暮らしている良寛、人恋しいのだ。

Meaning of Tanka and Ryōkan's heart:
　During winter, I am staying in my humble hut covered with snow in the snowy country Echigo. No one comes or goes, and there are no traces of coming and going all season.

　No one visited Ryōkan in the winter. He lived alone at his humble hut wishing someone would visit.

100	I can hardly wait for spring,
	so I will begin to count
	from now on
	いついつか春を待ちわび数へをり
	Itsuitsu ka haru wo machiwabi kazoe wori

元歌   今よりはいつかいつかとあづさ弓
　　　　　まだ来ぬ春を数へて待たむ

Imayori wa/ itsuka itsuka to/ adusayumi

mada konu haru wo/ kazoete matan

歌意と良寛の心情：　まだ来ない春を、今からいつやって来るのかと、指折り数えて待つとしよう。

梅の花が咲き出す春が好きで、待ちきれない良寛。

Meaning of Tanka and Ryōkan's heart:

Spring hasn't yet come, so I will wait and count the days until it arrives.

Ryōkan can hardly wait for spring to arrive which means plum blossoms will begin to bloom.

おわりに

　2024年、私は八十八歳－米寿－を迎えた。

　米寿は長生きしたと祝ってもらう風習があるが、今や百年時代、周りを見ても九十五歳を超える人がどんどん増えている。

　其の反面世界を見渡すと、多くの若者が国家権力により若くしてその命を失っている。権力者が好きな戦争によってである。多くの市民の方々が、子供もふくめ、その戦争に巻き込まれて命を落としている。

　更に私たち動物・植物を含め、生あるものが暮らすこの地球が、人類の生活による環境汚染のため、その生命の存続に危険性が忍び寄っている。

　国連では戦争、環境問題についていろいろ討議はされているも、大国のエゴイズムも加わり、実効性のあるものは生まれてこない。

　人類史始まって以来続いている戦争は無くすることは困難と思われる。

　せめて地球環境の改善を図り、次世代の人々の負担を軽減させるためには、現代人は今の驕りある生活を改善しなければならない。

　良寛さんは自然を慈しみ、人々には慈愛の心を持ち、質素な生活の中にも楽しみを見出し、己に厳しく、平穏に七十四歳の人生を過ごした。

　人生百年になるでしょう。それ故に良寛さんの生き方が多くの人々に影響を与えるようになればと願っています。

Epilogue

In the year 2024, I celebrated my eighty-eighth birthday.

In Japan, there is the familiar custom that a person who is eighty-eight is celebrated as having lived a long life by families and acquaintances.

Now it is said that a one hundred year's age celebration might be coming. Actually, there has been a gradual increase of people over ninety-five years old around myself.

But at the same time, looking out over the world many young people lost their lives by the wars under the power of the government. In history, the people in authority have almost always liked wars. Many civilians, including children, have been killed involved with wars.

Moreover, all of the living things on this earth are now threatened with the risk of their lives by the environmental destruction caused due to human lives.

Though it has been much discussed in the United Nations about wars and environmental problems, no useful solutions have been created by the egoism of the great nations.

It is thought difficult that the wars in history, having been continued until today, will come to an end before long.

At the very least, all people now living on this earth have to improve the damaged environment of the earth for the next generation, so that we should get out from the present luxurious lives damaging the earth.

A monk Ryōkan passed away at the age of seventy-four having lived a peaceful life, loving nature, associating with many people with loving and warm heart, and having joyful works in humble and strict lives.

Human life may last one hundred years. Therefore, I hope that Ryōkan's way of life may influence a great number of people.

Tatsuo Ebe

謝　　辞

　この本の上梓に当たり、多くの方々からご指導、ご援助を頂いた。厚くお礼申し上げます。

　この本の発行所である（株）考古堂書店　会長　柳本雄司様には、この本の完成には欠かせなかった方々のご紹介を頂いた。

　北嶋藤郷様　敬和学園大学名誉教授
　　　　本書の校正・校閲協力者
　Matthew Diaz 様　新潟清心女子中学高等学校教諭
　　　　本書の英文校閲協力者
　小林春規様　版画家
　　　　本書の表紙と中扉の版画のご提供
　赤塚　一様　風景写真家
　　　　本書の挿絵の風景写真のご提供

　尚、翻案された俳句の添削は大学時代の学友である神山　務君（小田原市で小児科医として活躍、俳人、小田原市の俳句協会の理事）にお願いした。

Acknowledgments

　I would like to express my deepest thanks to persons who were necessary for publishing this book.

　Mr. Yūji Yagishita, the chairperson of the board of directors of Kōkodō Publishing Company, introduced necessary persons for completing this book.

　Mr. Fujisato Kitajima, professor emeritus at Keiwa College, English and American Literature: He is one of proofreaders of this book.

　Mr. Matthew Diaz, teacher of English at Niigata Seishin Girls Junior & Senior High School: He checked and corrected the English part of this book as one of the proofreaders.

　Mr. Haruki Kobayashi, woodblock-print artist, provided woodblock-prints used as the frontispiece and the inner piece of this book.

　Mr. Hajime Akatsuka, landscape photo artist, provided landscape photographs used in this book.

Moreover, the Haiku adapted from Ryōkan's Tanka poems were corrected by Dr. Tsutomu Kamiyama (pediatrician, haiku poet, my school friend at Niigata University, and now a director of Odawara Haiku Society).

参考資料　Bibliography

『良寛の名歌百選』　選・解説　谷川敏朗　写真　小林新一（考古堂書店）

『良寛　こころのうた』〈三部作〉　全国良寛会（新潟日報事業社）

『校本　良寛歌集』　横山　英（考古堂書店）

『良寛百科』　加藤僖一（新潟日報事業社）

『良寛の生涯と芸術－慈愛に満ちた心－』　小島正芳（考古堂書店）

『温良にして厳正　良寛さん～幸せに生きる心』　中川幸次（考古堂書店）

『華厳の愛　貞心尼と良寛の真実』　本間　明（考古堂書店）

『良寛の清貧の生き方と慈愛の心』　本間　明（野積良寛研究所）

『声に出して読みたい良寛の歌』　本間　明（野積良寛研究所）

『美しい日本の私』　川端康成（講談社現代新書）

『良寛　短歌・俳句選』　RYŌKAN: SELECTED TANKA・HAIKU Sanford
　　　　Goldstein, Shigeo Mizuguchi and Fujisato Kitajima（考古堂書店）

『大愚良寛（渡辺秀英　校註)』　相馬御風（考古堂書店）

『Ryōkan the Great Fool』　Misao Kodama and Hikosaku Yanagishima
　　　　　　　　　　　　　　　　　　　　　　　　　　　（私家版）

著 者 略 歴

1936年（昭和11年）10月　新潟県長岡市に生まれる
1963年（昭和38年）3月　新潟大学医学部卒業
1968年（昭和43年）3月　新潟大学大学院卒業　内科学専攻
以降、呼吸器内科医として2018年まで診療に従事する

［著書］　医学書「Fine Structure of Human Cells and Tissues」
　　　　　故　小林　繁　名古屋大学医学部教授　共著（医学書院）
　　　　　随筆集「大自然に遊ぶ」（考古堂書店）
　　　　　句集　「越新潟の自然の中で」（アドマドネット社）
　　　　　句集　「短歌を俳句に詠み替える　百人一首と良寛」（考古堂書店）

［受賞］　1974年　日本臨床電子顕微鏡学会賞
　　　　　2000年　新潟県民文化祭で新潟出版文化賞　文芸部門賞
　　　　　2009年　結核予防会全国大会で功労賞

```
良寛の名歌を俳句(英文・和文)に翻案
        2025年1月20日発行

    著　者    江部　達夫
    発行人    柳本　和貴
    発行所    株式会社　考古堂書店
            〒951-8063　新潟市中央区古町4番町563番地
    電　話    025-229-4058（出版部直通）
    FAX     025-224-8654
    印刷所    株式会社　ウィザップ
```

ISBN 978-4-87499-018-6　C0092